Kate Fortune's Journal Entry

That old clapboard New England home holds such special memories for me. I'm so pleased that my granddaughter Jane and her son, Cody, are making good use of it. She and her little boy have had a rough time of it. When Cody's father abandoned Jane before Cody was even born, I knew the road ahead would be difficult. But her family has always been there to support her. Now I hope some of the "magic" of the house weaves its spell around her. And that she'll finally be able to discover true love....

A LETTER FROM THE AUTHOR

Dear Reader,

It isn't often I get the chance to speak directly to
you at the beginning of a book, and I'm so glad my
editors at Silhouette gave me that opportunity with
A Husband in Time. I'm very excited to be a part of
this special series, and was even more thrilled when I
learned the *type* of story I would be asked to write.
When you read it, I'm sure you'll see why.

A Husband in Time is my twelfth novel with Silhouette.
From the very first book, I've felt the warmth of those of
you who read them. Through the letters you send me, and
the books you buy, you let me know that the work I put
in to these stories is worth the effort, because someone,
somewhere, is getting pleasure from reading them. That's
what makes it all worthwhile. And it's also what keeps me
punching away at the keyboard, day after day. As long as
you keep enjoying them, I'll keep writing them.

Happy reading!

Maggie Shayne

MAGGIE SHAYNE
A Husband in Time

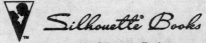

Published by Silhouette Books
America's Publisher of Contemporary Romance

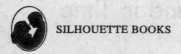

SILHOUETTE BOOKS

A HUSBAND IN TIME

Copyright © 1997 by Harlequin Books S.A.

ISBN 0-373-38908-6

Special thanks and acknowledgment are given to Maggie Shayne
for her contribution to the FORTUNE'S CHILDREN series.

Visit Silhouette Books at www.eHarlequin.com

Printed in U.S.A.

MAGGIE SHAYNE,

a *USA TODAY* bestselling author whom *Romantic Times* calls "brilliantly inventive," has written more than twenty-five novels for Silhouette.

Maggie has won numerous awards, including two *Romantic Times* Career Achievement Awards. A five-time finalist for the Romance Writers of America's prestigious RITA® Award, Maggie also writes mainstream contemporary fantasy and romantic suspense for MIRA Books, and has contributed story lines to network daytime soap operas.

She lives in rural Otselic, New York, with her husband, Rick, with whom she shares five beautiful daughters, two English bulldogs and two grandchildren.

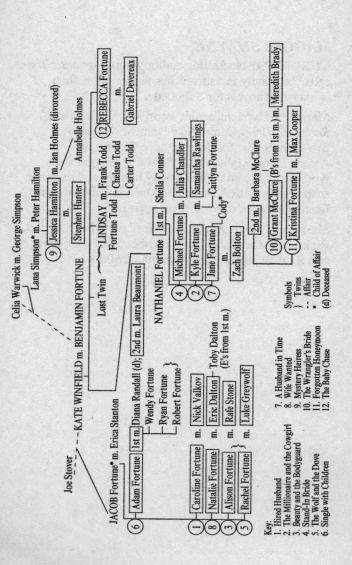

Celia Warwick m. George Simpson

Lana Simpson* m. Peter Hamilton

Jessica Hamilton ⑨ m. Ian Holmes (divorced)

Annabelle Holmes

LINDSAY m. Frank Todd

Stephen Hunter m.

Fortune Todd ⎰ Chelsea Todd
                ⎱ Carter Todd

⑫ REBECCA Fortune
m.
Gabriel Devereax

KATE WINFIELD m. BENJAMIN FORTUNE

Lost Twin

NATHANIEL Fortune 1st m. Sheila Conner

Michael Fortune ④ m. Julia Chandler

Kyle Fortune ②

Jane Fortune ⑦ m. Samantha Rawlings
                    ⎰ Caitlyn Fortune
                    ⎱ Cody*

Zach Bolton

2nd m. Barbara McClure

Grant McClure ⑩ (B's from 1st m.) m. Meredith Brady

Kristina Fortune ⑪ m. Max Cooper

Joe Stover

JACOB Fortune* m. Erica Stanton

Adam Fortune ⑥

Diana Randall (d); 2nd m. Laura Beaumont

1st m. ⎰ Wendy Fortune
       ⎱ Ryan Fortune }
         Robert Fortune }

Toby Dalton
Eric Dalton (E's from 1st m.)

Caroline Fortune ① m. Nick Valkov

Natalie Fortune ⑧ m. Eric Dalton

Alison Fortune ③ ⎰ m. Rafe Stone
Rachel Fortune ⑤ ⎱ m. Luke Greywolf

Symbols
⎰⎱ Twins
-- Affair
* Child of Affair
(d) Deceased

Key:
1. Hired Husband
2. The Millionaire and the Cowgirl
3. Beauty and the Bodyguard
4. Stand-In Bride
5. The Wolf and the Dove
6. Single with Children
7. A Husband in Time
8. Wife Wanted
9. Mystery Heiress
10. The Wrangler's Bride
11. Forgotten Honeymoon
12. The Baby Chase

FORTUNE'S Children™

Meet the Fortunes—three generations of a family with a legacy of wealth, influence and power. As they unite to face an unknown enemy, shocking family secrets are revealed...and passionate new romances are ignited.

JANE FORTUNE: The single mother secretly dreams of finding a husband, and a father for her six-year-old son. She has almost given up hope until a mystery man comes to her out of nowhere....

ZACH BOLTON: He can't explain who he is, or where he's come from. He feels at home with Jane and her son, but can he stay with them—forever?

MONICA MALONE: She now owns major shares in Fortune Cosmetics. What further havoc will she create to claim the rest of the Fortune wealth?

JAKE FORTUNE: The hardworking family man is hiding a deep, dark secret. Is he in cahoots with Monica? Once his secret is discovered, the Fortune empire might come tumbling down....

NATALIE FORTUNE: Kindhearted schoolteacher. Could a farmhouse and St. Bernard inherited from her grandmother lead to the exciting romance with a dashing man she's been dreaming of?

LIZ JONES — CELEBRITY GOSSIP

Is anyone but me wondering why Jake Fortune sold Monica Malone sizable shares of stock in Fortune Cosmetics? After all, Monica is just a faded starlet coasting on her former glory and fame. Do you suppose Jake and Monica are having a torrid affair? Or perhaps the shrewd Monica is holding some juicy secret over Jake's head and blackmailing him? Rumors are running rampant.

The rest of the Fortunes are up in arms. Now Monica owns a big piece of the business, and who knows what type of control she'll want to wield.

This is going to be a battle to the bitter end. And I'm putting my money on the Fortunes!

One

Six-year-old Benjamin Bolton rested against a stack of pillows in his bedroom—the first room on the left, right at the top of the stairs. He couldn't get out of bed very often, not at all without his father's help. But Father had turned his bed around and tied the curtains open so that Ben could see the sky as he lay there. And tonight, as he stared up at the sparkling night sky, he saw a shooting star...and then another, and a third. They zipped across their blue-black home, leaving white-hot trails, and though it wasn't very scientific at all, Benjamin closed his eyes and wished with everything in him.

"Three shooting stars, that's three wishes for me. I wish..." He bit his lip, thinking hard to be sure he'd word the wishes right, and not waste them. "I wish to be well again, so I can run and play outdoors, and ride my pony, and not die like they all think I'm going to, even though they don't say it out loud."

He drew a breath, heard the wheezy sound it made as it whistled into his weakened lungs. His head hurt. He ached most everywhere, and he was dog-tired. His eyes tried to close, but he forced them open. This was important, and he still had two wishes to go.

"I wish for a mother. A real mother, who will love me and read to me... And who isn't afraid of bull-frogs, like Mrs. Haversham is." He smiled after he made the wish, because he was sure he'd worded it just right.

Licking his lips, Benjamin squeezed his eyes tight, and made the third wish, the one he'd been wishing for all his life. "And I wish for a big brother. I promise I won't ever fight with him or tease. I would like for him to be smart, and brave, and strong, just like my father. I'll even share my pony with him."

Ben opened his eyes, gazing out the window. No trace of the stars remained. But they'd been there. He'd seen them. And now an odd, warm feeling settled over him, just like a big woolly blanket. Somehow, he just knew everything was going to be all right.

August 4, 1997

Cody Fortune glanced up from the laptop computer his mom had given him for his tenth birthday, turning his head just in time to see the three shooting stars arching over their car as it rolled over the narrow, deserted roads of Maine, heading for the coast and their new home.

"Wow," he whispered, craning his neck for a better look. Of all the things he'd seen on this trip from Minnesota, this was the most incredible. Three at once. It had to be an anomaly.

"Did you see that, Mom?"

"What?"

"Three shooting stars, right in a row!"

She smiled at him, only taking her eyes from the road for a second. "So, why don't you make a wish? Or are you too skeptical for that?"

Cody Fortune was far too intelligent to believe in any such thing as wishing on stars. But he knew his mom didn't like him taking life too seriously, and some touch of whimsy moved him to close his eyes and whisper the things that had been on his mind the most lately. "I wish I had a dad," he said softly. "And a little brother, because it gets so darn boring being an only child. We'd have great times together. And I wish…" He licked his lips, opened his eyes and stared up at the sky. His eyes watered just a little bit, but he blinked them dry again. "I wish for my mom to be happy. Really happy. 'Cause I know she isn't. I can't remember when she was."

He lowered his head, and his mother's soft hand stroked his hair. "Of course I'm happy, Cody. I have you, and a new house in a small town, just like I've always wanted. What more could I need?"

Cody smirked. He knew better, of course, but he'd never get her to admit her life was less than perfect. "You realize I've just wished on three hunks of burned-out rock, don't you?"

"It was still generous of you to use up a whole wish on me."

He shrugged and turned to the laptop again. It wasn't so bad that he'd lapsed into childish fantasies for a second there. It was like his mom was always saying, he was still a kid, even if he did have the brain of a full-grown nuclear physicist.

"So, have you thought about what I told you?" he asked, and saw her brows rise.

"About what, Cody?"

Cody sighed. When he spent the weekend with his grandparents, he'd stumbled on something he knew must be important, but his mother, as usual, couldn't care less about the family business. "What I overheard when Grandpa took me to work with him last week. Don't you remember? That witch Monica was there, and—"

"Cody, that isn't very nice."

"So? Neither is Monica. Anyway, she was being really nasty to Aunt Tracey. Said she knew some secret, and she'd tell if Tracey and her boyfriend, what's his name—? Wayne. Yeah, that's it. Monica said she wanted them to go away, or she'd tell some secret."

Jane shrugged. "I wouldn't worry about it, Cody. We all know Monica's been wanting to get her hands on the business. She probably sees Aunt Tracey as one more competitor for it."

"Yeah, but Aunt Tracey only just found out she *was* a Fortune."

"If she's a Fortune, Cody, she can handle empty threats from Monica Malone." She sent him a sideways glance. "This is just one more example of why I want no part of the family business, pal. All the scratching and clawing and fighting to hold on to it." She gazed out the window at the rugged coastline as they passed it. "It's going to be so much better here."

Cody sighed. It was no use talking to his mother about business. She just didn't care. He stared at the dark ocean, and the whitecapped waves crashing to the shore, and then he thought maybe she was right.

It was kind of pretty here. "So how much longer till we get there?"

"I think… I think this is— Oh, my, Cody, this *is* the place. Look at it!"

Cody looked up at the house their headlights illuminated as the car turned into the gravel drive. "Looks like something out of a Stephen King novel."

"Isn't it *great?*"

He grimaced at his mother's enthusiasm as she brought the car to a halt and killed the engine.

"I thought you liked Stephen King novels," she said.

"Yeah, but I don't want to live in one."

She smiled at him. Then he turned his gaze to the house once again, and froze. From the corner of his eye, he'd seen some kind of flash in an upstairs window. Like…lightning or something. His mom was already opening her door, but he put a hand on her arm, stopping her. "I think…somebody's in there."

"What?" She frowned and looked where he pointed. "I don't see anything."

"Maybe it was just a reflection." But he didn't think so. He folded up the laptop and pulled his penlight from his pocket. He never went far without it— not that it would make a very good weapon, but at least he'd be able to see whatever horrible creature sneaked up on him. "Better let me go in first, Mom, just in case."

She ruffled his hair, which he hated. "My hero," she said, but he could tell she wasn't one bit nervous about going into that big, empty, dark house. She must be nuts.

Headlights spilled through the rear windshield, and Cody turned to see a second vehicle bounding over the gravel drive. A police car. He bit his lip before he could say, "Thank God!" Though he was still a bit nervous. In Stephen King novels, the small-town sheriffs of Maine never failed to be good guys, but they usually got killed off pretty early on, leaving the innocent mother—and her son, who knew all along something wasn't quite right, but who couldn't get anyone to listen—to fend for themselves.

Sure enough, a reed-thin man in a gray uniform with a shiny badge, stepped out of the car, and came over just as Mom stepped out of theirs.

"Quigly O'Donnell, ma'am. You must be Ms. Fortune. You're right on time." He had the same accent as the old man who'd lived across the street from the main characters in *Pet Semetary*. Cody shivered.

"Call me Jane," his mom said, and shook the sheriff's hand. "And this is my son, Cody."

Cody nodded, but didn't shake. He was too busy watching the house. "I thought I saw something up there," he said, pointing, hoping the sheriff would go against character and check it out, hoping the guy would survive the experience.

"Ayuh, I wouldn't worry about that, son. Probably just the ghost."

"Ghost?"

"Some say the ghost of Zachariah Bolton still rattles around the old place. Not that I'd give it much credence, mind you. It's just a tale the old folks like to tell now and again. Gives 'em something to talk about over checkers, it does."

"Checkers," Cody said, raising a brow. "Gee, Mom, thanks for bringing me to such a cultural mecca."

"Mind your manners, Cody. Sheriff O'Donnell, if you brought the key along, I'll—"

"Got it right here," he said, and the last word sounded like "hee-ya." Mom would call that accent charming and say it was local "flavor." Cody found it irritating as all get-out. The sheriff held up a big old key on a brass ring. Like a jail-cell key from an old western. Or the key to the dungeons in a horror flick. Cody felt the tone slipping from King to Poe. This was not a good sign. "I'll help you with your things, if you like. Power's been turned on, and everything should be ready for you."

"That was kind of you, Sheriff."

"Yeah," Cody put in. "I'm glad to know we've got pow-uh."

His mom's elbow dug into his ribs, but the doomed sheriff didn't seem to notice Cody's mimicry. He just nodded. "Least I could do for your grandmother, ma'am. Kate Fortune was one hell of a lady, if you'll pardon the expression. When she asked me to watch after the place for her, I was more than happy to do it. Pity we've lost her now."

Jane nodded. "I miss her terribly." She slipped an arm around Cody's shoulders and squeezed. "We both do."

The sheriff nodded, cleared his throat. "Well, come on and follow me. I'll show you around. And while I'm at it, I'll tell you all about our town's one and only claim to fame. This place's original owner, and resident ghost, if you believe in that kind'a thing.

Zachariah Bolton.'' He walked as he spoke, in that
slow, lazy pattern that left every sentence sounding
like a question. They followed him up the porch's
wide steps and across it to the front door, which was
tall, and dark, and to Cody's way of thinking just a
little bit scary.

Then Quigly O'Donnell opened the front door, and
he decided he'd been wrong. It was a *lot* scary.

Quigly O'Donnell snapped on a light.

It was *fabulous!* Everything Jane had ever wanted
in a home was in this house. Oh, she knew most of
her family thought her hopelessly old-fashioned, but
she wasn't fond of modern society and all its trap-
pings. Modern-day values were what had landed her
pregnant and alone ten years ago, and that shock had
gone a long way toward guiding Jane to her own
perhaps outmoded system of morality.

This house was the embodiment of the life she
wanted for her and Cody. A simple, old-fashioned
life. With one notable exception. There would be no
father in this traditional American family. Jane was
mom and dad and everything in between. Everyone
said she couldn't do it all, that she was pushing herself too hard. But she could. And she'd do it without
her family's money. She wanted no part of the family
business or the wealth that went with it. It was a rat
race, everyone fighting to hold on to their share of
the pie and always worrying about someone trying
to take it from them. No. That wasn't anything she
wanted to be involved with.

This, though—this would be perfect.

''I never thought my modern-minded grandmother

had a clue what to make of me," she whispered as she moved through the modest entry hall and into the Gothic living room, with its high ceilings and intricate, darkly stained woodwork. "But Grandma Kate knew me better than I ever imagined. She must have, to have left me this place." All around them, furniture stood draped in white sheets, like an army of ghosts.

"And that guest house out front will be perfect for my antique shop." She couldn't stop smiling. The place was her dream come true.

"The house isn't the half of it, ma'am," Sheriff O'Donnell offered. "It's the history that goes along with it that makes it so special." He'd carried in two of their suitcases, and he set them on the hardwood floor. "You've heard of quinaria fever, of course?"

"Heard of it?" Jane glanced behind her, but Cody was already off exploring nooks and crannies, flashing his ever-present penlight into closets and cupboards. Her heart twisted a little in her chest at the mere mention of the disease. "I nearly lost my son from it," she said quietly. "He was exposed as a baby. Thankfully, we caught it in time."

Frowning, the sheriff tilted his head. "Well, now, if that don't beat all..." Then he shrugged. "Hell of a coincidence, ma'am, if you'll pardon the expression."

"Why's that, Sheriff?"

"Well, Zachariah Bolton was the man responsible for finding the cure. Tryptonine, you know. Same drug we use today, with a few modifications, of course. If it hadn't been for him— Ah, now here's the dining room. Floor-to-ceiling hardwood cupboards on two walls. See there? Same as in the kitchen. And the ones here on the wall in between..." He opened a cupboard door, left it wide, then meandered into the kitchen. Opening the cupboard from that side, he peered through at her. "See that? Accessible from either side."

"That's very nice." But she was more interested in the tale he'd been telling before.

Cody joined them then, having heard the tail end of the sheriff's comments. "You're dead wrong about tryptonine, Sheriff," he said, then grinned innocently at his mom and added, "if you'll pardon the expression."

"Cody!"

"Come on, Mom. Everyone learns this stuff in fourth grade. The quinaria virus was cured by Bausch and Waterson in 1898."

Jane scrunched her eyebrows and shook her head. "Are you a walking encyclopedia, or what?"

He shrugged and looked past her to Sheriff O'Donnell.

"Well, now, that's a bright young fellow you have there, Ms. Fortune. Cody, is it? Well, Cody, m'boy, you have part of it right. But you don't know the whole tale. Did you know, for instance, that Wilhelm Bausch and Eli Waterson spent most of their time competing against one another? Great researchers, sure enough. But more focused on getting the jump on each other than on the importance of their work. Blinded by ambition, you might say."

Jane saw Cody's eyes narrow suspiciously. But he listened.

"It was their friend Zachariah Bolton who finally

brought them together. And only by working together were they able to find the cure.'' He waved a hand to indicate that they should follow him and turned back toward the living room, then headed up the stairs. ''Come on, I want to show you something.''

Jane knew she was grinning like a loon, but she couldn't help herself. ''Isn't this great, Codester? A house complete with a ghost and a historical past?''

''Mom, you're too into history. Get with the nineties, willya?''

''Yeah, yeah. Hurry up, I want to hear the rest of this.'' She followed her son, noticing the way he paused just outside the door of the room at the top of the stairs. He stood still for a moment, staring at that door. Then shivered and rubbed the back of his neck with one hand.

''You okay, pal?''

''Yeah. Sure, fine. C'mon.''

Sheriff O'Donnell headed into a bedroom farther down the hall, snapped on a light and waved his arm with a flourish when they entered.

Jane caught her breath. ''My God,'' she whispered, blinking at the portrait on the far wall. ''It looks like a Rockwell!'' She moved closer, ran her fingertips lovingly over the ornate frame, then touched the work itself. ''But it can't be. This has to be at least a hundred years old.''

''You have a fine eye, Jane.''

''I know antiques,'' she said with a shrug. ''It's my business. This is unsigned. Do you know who did it?''

''Ayuh, unsigned, and no, I don't know who the

artist was,'' O'Donnell said. ''But it's yours, along with everything else in the house. Including the old safe in the attic, still locked up. Might even be some of Zachariah Bolton's old notes and such tucked away in there. Yours to do with as you please, just as your grandmother's will specified.''

Jane couldn't take her eyes from the portrait on the wall. A very Rockwellian painting of a dark-haired man, eyes passionate and intense, hair rumpled, white shirt unbuttoned at the neck. In one hand he held a small contraption with springs and wires sprouting in all directions, and in the other a tiny screwdriver. Gold-rimmed glasses perched on his nose, and those piercing, deep brown eyes stared through them at his work. And beside him, right beside him, dressed in identical clothes—though in a much smaller size—sat a little boy who couldn't be more than five or six. He had carrot-colored curls and bright green eyes, and he was tinkering with a tiny screwdriver of his own. The two sat so close they had to be touching. And the connection between them was so strong it was palpable, though they weren't even looking at one another. At the bottom of the painting was a single word: Inventor.

''That there is Zachariah Bolton, ma'am,'' Sheriff O'Donnell told her. ''And the boy is his son, Benjamin.''

''Benjamin,'' she whispered. ''That was my grandfather's name and this child looks enough like Cody to be his...'' Jane's voice trailed off.

''Little brother,'' Cody finished, stepping farther into the room.

''Bolton was a friend and colleague to Wilhelm

Bausch and Eli Waterson. In fact, they both said publicly that they considered him one of the greatest scientific minds of their time. One of the few things they agreed on, it was. Well, sir, when little Benjamin died of quinaria fever—''

Jane gasped, her eyes snapping back to the mischievous green ones in the painting. ''Oh, no. That sweet little boy?''

''Yes, ma'am. And the day the boy passed, Zachariah Bolton went plumb out of his mind. The grief was too much for him, they say. Locked himself in the boy's bedroom and refused to let anyone in. When they finally forced the door, he was long gone. And he'd taken the poor little fellow's body right along with him. Bolton was never heard from again. Now, Bausch and Waterson were distraught enough over it that they vowed to find a cure for the disease that took little Benjamin. And by heaven, that's just what they did.''

Jane blinked away the inexplicable tears that came to her eyes as she heard the story. ''That's so incredibly sad.''

''Yes, ma'am, that it is. I can take that painting down, store it somewhere, if it's going to bother you.''

''No,'' she answered quickly. ''No, leave it right here.'' Her eyes found those of the inventor again, and she could almost feel his pain.

''The place hasn't changed much over the years,'' the sheriff mused. ''Aside from some fresh paint and paper, it's almost exactly the way Bolton left it. Almost as if it's been...waiting...or something.''

Jane frowned at the man. "But it's been a century."

"Ayuh. After Bolton vanished, his friends, Bausch and Waterson looked after the place. Kept the taxes paid up and so on, always insisting Bolton would come back someday. Course, he never did." Quigly shrugged and heaved a sigh. "The house was left alone for a short while, of course, after the two men passed. Went to the town for taxes, and naturally the town kept it up, hoping to sell it one day. Never did, though. Not until your Grandma Kate came along. And even when she bought it, she refused to change a thing."

Jane could understand that reluctance to change this place. It had a soul to it, as if it were a living entity—or was that the lingering presence of the long-dead scientist she felt in every room?

"Hey, Mom?"

She turned, surprised that Cody's voice came from a distance and not right behind her, where he'd been standing only seconds ago. "Codester? Where are you?" She stepped out of the master bedroom, into the hall. Cody stood two doors down, in front of that room at the top of the stairs. The one that seemed to have given him a scare before.

"I want this room, if it's okay with you," he said. Frowning, Jane went to where he stood near the now open door. He looked in at a rather ordinary-looking bedroom, with no furniture to speak of, and nothing exceptional about it except for the huge marble fireplace on one wall.

"I kind of thought this room...gave you the willies. Isn't this where you thought you saw something before?''

''That's why I want it,'' Cody said. He looked at her and shrugged. ''If there is some kind of ghost hanging out around here, I want to know about it.''

''Gonna analyze it until you convince it it can't possibly exist?''

''Maybe,'' he said, grinning. ''So when are the movers gonna get here with my Nintendo?''

Two

Thunder rumbled and growled in the distance, and Zachariah got up from the chair where he'd been keeping constant vigil to light the oil lamp on his son's bedside table. Benjamin had always been afraid of thunderstorms. Just as Zach fitted the glass chimney into place, Ben stirred, as Zach had known he would.

"Father... Oh. You're right here."

"Where else would I be?"

"Working on the device, of course. You waste an awful lot of time sitting here with me, you know."

"I like sitting with you." Thunder cracked again, and Benjamin reached for his father's hand, found it, and held tight.

"There, now. No need to be afraid, son. You know thunder can't hurt you."

"That doesn't make it any less noisy, though," Benjamin said, quite reasonably. "How much longer will it last, Father? It's been storming all night."

Zachariah pulled the gold watch from his vest pocket, opened it and then turned its face toward his son. "It's only 9:08, my boy. It hasn't been storming all night, only a couple of hours. And it will end any time now, I'm cer—''

His words were cut off by the loudest, sharpest crack yet, this one so loud it even made Zachariah jump a bit. At the same instant, the night sky beyond Benjamin's window was ripped apart by a blinding, jagged streak.

''Father, the lightning! It's hit something!''

Zach moved to the edge of the bed and gathered his son in his arms. ''There now...'' he said. ''It wasn't as close as it seemed.'' But he kept his gaze focused on that one spot in the night where the lightning seemed to have struck. And as he watched, he rocked his son, whispered to him, stroked his hair.

Within seconds, a pinprick of light danced in the distant sky. And then it began to grow, and spread, until Zach recognized it for what it was. A fire. And from what he could see, it was the old Thomas barn, nearly three miles away, that had been hit, and that was now burning. No great loss. It was an old, decrepit building and hadn't been used in years. The only thing inside, so far as he knew, was some musty old hay.

Benjamin fell asleep in Zachariah's arms, and Zach remained right where he was all night long, holding his precious child and watching the growing blaze in the distance. Soon it illuminated the entire night sky. The barn was old, tinder-dry, and had gone up like a matchstick.

Zach ought to be working. He knew he should, for so very much depended on the success of the current experiment. And he was so close. So close.

Right now, though, Benjamin needed him. And right now he couldn't bring himself to leave.

But as the sun rose high the next morning, and spirals of smoke still rose from the charred remains of the old Thomas barn, Zach gently tried to extricate himself from the bed without disturbing Benjamin. And he did. A bit too easily. As he got to his feet, it hit him that, sick as he was, Benjamin was normally a very light sleeper. He should have at least stirred when Zach got up from the bed.

A cold chill crept up his spine as he turned to face his son, who hadn't so much as stirred in his sleep all night.

And then Zachariah Bolton's heart froze over. He shook Ben's frail shoulders gently, tapped his pale cheek. But there was no response. His son had slipped into a coma. The state that marked the final stages of his illness. Death was only twenty-four hours away now, perhaps less.

There was no more time. None whatsoever. He must act now, and if the experiment had side effects, then so be it. He'd suffer whatever he must in order to save his son's life.

He reached into his vest, and removed the device from its pocket. There was no longer any reason to stay by his son's side. Benjamin wouldn't wake again. Not unless... Not unless this worked.

Leaning over the bed, he stroked his son's coppery curls, kissed his forehead. "I'll be gone for a little while, my Ben. But I'll try to arrange it so it's only an instant for you. I don't want to leave you, but I must to get you healthy again. Understand?"

Benjamin's auburn lashes rested on his chalk-white cheeks, and his breath wheezed in and out of his rail-thin body.

Zach straightened and pushed his hands through his hair. He looked like hell. He knew it without a glimpse at the looking glass. His clothes were rumpled, vest unbuttoned and gaping. The thin black tie he'd worn the day before hung loose from his collar. He'd planned, though. There was a small satchel in Benjamin's wardrobe, with a change of clothes and the things he'd need. Including proof, should he be questioned. He took a moment to retrieve the satchel. No time to change. Not now. Ben could very well expire while his father worried over such trivial matters. But once Zach was gone, time would virtually stand still for his son. Time enough to bathe then. If he was displeasing to those he met, well, too bad for them. Not that he was likely to meet anyone at all. Each time he'd opened the portal, it had shown him an empty, unlived-in version of his own house. Not that he cared right now who he might meet, or what they might think of him.

He wasn't thinking of himself. Not at all. He wasn't thinking of society, either, or of the repercussions he knew full well might come from his tampering with nature this way. He flatly refused to consider those. The only thing on Zachariah Bolton's mind was his son. His precious Benjamin. The only thing that mattered right now was finding a way to save his child's fragile life. The child who was, right now, precariously close to death. And he could do it. Zachariah Bolton could do it. He could travel backward through time. He could go back to a time before his son had been exposed to the killing virus that was trying so hard to take him. And when he arrived there, he'd take Benjamin away, somewhere safe. So that when the virus pummelled Rockwell, Ben would be far away. He'd never be exposed. And when the danger had passed, he'd bring Ben home safe and sound. He'd never become sick. He'd never die. He'd be all right. Zach would return here, to this time, to find his son healthy and well again. With no memory of having been sick at all.

Zach's heartbeat escalated as he pointed the device toward *that spot* in the very center of his son's bedroom. He had no idea what the spot was. A wrinkle in the fabric of time. A rent. Whatever it was, it was only here, in this room, and he suspected it had been here, hovering in the air above the ground, even before the house was built. He'd attempted the experiment in numerous locations, but here and here alone had he found success. One night, when he'd been working in here so as to be with his ailing child, he'd discovered the portal purely by accident.

With his thumb, he depressed the initiator button. And a pinprick of light appeared in midair, at the room's center. Holding the device steady, he turned the expander dial, and the light grew bigger, brighter, until it was a glowing sphere that extended beyond the ceiling and the floor. A mist-filled, glowing orb. But even that began to change. The mists cleared and took on forms, and in moments Zach was looking into what appeared to be a huge mirror. And the mirror reflected this very room back at him. Only in another time. He could clearly see that the wallpaper was different, and the curtains in the windows were different, and the furnishings. Everything. Right down to the small body bundled beneath the covers in the bed. Benjamin? Before he was taken ill, when he was well and strong and healthy? This was going to work. It was going to work!

He only hoped it didn't kill him. Every test so far indicated there would be side effects. The tea cup Zach had pushed through the portal a few days ago had shattered. He'd made adjustments to the device and tried again. The apple he sent through had withered, and he'd made still more changes. The mouse...the mouse had died. And though Zach had recalculated and made even more changes, he couldn't be certain he had it right this time. So, yes, there might be side effects. Serious ones. He just didn't know what they would be, yet. But—he smiled a little—he was about to find out. "You're going to be all right, Benjamin. I swear to you. You'll be well again!" And Zachariah Bolton stepped into the light, and promptly felt a post wallop him right between the eyes.

Jane Fortune couldn't sleep. There was simply too much on her mind. Oh, not the house. The house was perfect, she'd known that the second she saw it. The aging but elegant Victorian, standing like a guardian of the sea. The rocky Maine shoreline below. The songs of the waves that would sing her to sleep under ordinary circumstances.

Her new antique shop—Jane smiled at the words—was now a reality. She'd researched the area, made new contacts and stocked up on local finds. She'd been open for several weeks now, and business was brisk. The guest house—a miniature copy of the main house, perched at its feet as if the house had given birth to a pup—was perfect, just as Jane had known it would be. Even the nearby town, appropriately named Rockwell, was picture-perfect. The epitome of the New England fantasy. A place time and progress seemed to have forgotten. It boasted a corner drugstore complete with a soda fountain and a barbershop with an old-fashioned candy-cane pole outside. When she walked along Rockwell's sidewalks, she half expected to round a corner and spot four men in flat-topped straw hats and handlebar mustaches singing about strolling through the park.

But as Grandma Kate used to say, when things seem too good to be true, look out, because they probably are. What if the business failed? What would she do then? Go running back to Minneapolis with her tail between her legs?

No. No, this move had been hard enough on Cody. She wouldn't uproot him again. She'd make this work, somehow. She had to, for her son's sake.

But financial worries were not the only things troubling Jane's mind tonight. She was more concerned about her son than about anything else. Cody's wish for a father had gnawed at her heart from the second he uttered it in the car that night. He was an intelligent child—gifted, the school officials called him. He knew he'd had a father once. But while Jane didn't believe in lying to her son, she hadn't told him the whole truth about Greg. He knew only that his father had been a talented musician who died when Cody was still a baby. She'd left out the rest. She'd never told Cody how taken in she'd been by Greg's idealism and sincerity, and the beauty and meaning behind the songs he wrote and played in clubs around Minneapolis. God, when she thought now about how quickly she'd fallen in love with him...

She'd been a fool. Greg's idealism had fled the second some L.A. big shot heard him play, and offered his band a recording contract. A pregnant young girlfriend who had made it clear she wanted no part of her family wealth, hadn't fit in with his new and improved plans. She wouldn't have wanted such a shallow and irresponsible man raising her son, anyway. She knew that now. But she also knew her son ached for the lack of a father in his life.

Oh, if only...

She looked wistfully at the painting on the wall beside her bed. Zachariah Bolton. His soft sable hair fell across his forehead, his brown eyes gleamed. The narrow black tie hung in two thin ribbons, and his vest was unbuttoned. The top of a gold watch peeked up from a small pocket.

The boy's resemblance to her own son struck her again, and she figured that might be a lot of the reason she liked the piece so much. The two sat very close to one another, at a wooden table with an oil lamp at either end. Each intent on his own work, but still, somehow, aware of the other. You could almost feel the love between them. Father and son, she'd have known that even without Quigly O'Donnell's narration. A father whose work meant the world to him, she thought, but who had never once allowed that work to come before his son.

If only Cody could have a father like that one.

Jane sighed, and relaxed deeper into her pillows. It was no use dreaming. She'd never find a man with those century-old values in the nineties. Not even in this nostalgic town. And she wouldn't settle for less. She didn't want another man whose career meant more to him than his own child. And she didn't want an ambitionless bum, or an immature, irresponsible overgrown kid, either.

She wanted...

Her gaze wandered back to the man in the painting. His full lips were parted just slightly, his strong jawline was taut, as if he were grating his teeth, and he was shoulder-to-shoulder with the little boy. The passion in his eyes was for his work. But it was intense enough to make her wonder if it had ever been there for a woman. His wife, the boy's mother, perhaps?

She smiled and shook her head. She was gifting the mysterious inventor with qualities he'd probably never had. The day after she and Cody moved in, Jane had made a trip to the Rockwell Public Library and borrowed several books on the town's history. The chapters on Bolton all read much the same. He'd been a notorious womanizer. The Don Juan of the nineteenth century, one author had dubbed him. None had mentioned his wife. Poor, long-suffering woman.

And yet that passion in the eyes of the inventor called to her.

Oh, but all this speculation was silly. The man was no longer living. And that probably wasn't passion at all in his eyes, but perhaps the beginnings of insanity. Once a man considered to be a genius, and far ahead of his time, Bolton had, the books claimed, crossed that fine line between brilliance and insanity.

And from what she'd read, Jane thought the madness had begun to take over long before the death of his precious son. Two accounts said that Bolton had claimed he'd discovered a way to travel through time. He'd been ridiculed for that claim, and soon after he'd refused to discuss it. Some said it was that ridicule that had sent him into seclusion, as much as the loss of his son. Whatever the reason, he'd dropped out of sight in 1890-something, never to be heard from again.

A shame. A crying shame.

"Mom! Mom, hurry!"

The alarm in Cody's voice pierced straight through every thought, to her very soul. Something was wrong. She jumped out of bed and ran into the hall, down it, and her heart was in her throat even before she exploded through his bedroom door and froze in place.

The moonlight spilled through the window and bathed the two forms in its pale, liquid glow. A rumpled, tousled man knelt on the floor, holding her son in his arms, so tightly she wondered if Cody could breathe. The man's back was toward Jane, and his shoulders shuddered and convulsed as if he were sobbing. Cody stared at her from the darkness, wide-eyed, as the man rocked him back and forth.

"My son," he kept whispering, his voice raw and coarse. "My boy, my son. Thank God..."

Jane's heart seemed to grind to a halt. Without a second's hesitation, she stepped into the room, snatched the baseball bat from where it leaned in the corner, lifted it and moved forward.

"Mom, no!"

Cody's shout made the lunatic who held him pause and stiffen, as if just realizing someone else had come into the room. And Jane hesitated. Instead of bringing the bat crashing down on his head, she just held it there, ready, poised. Her throat was so dry that the words sounded raspy and harsh when she said, "Let him go. Let him go, right now, or I swear…"

And he turned very slowly, still hugging Cody tight, to face her. The movement bringing him out of the light, so that his face was in shadow. His brows drew together, and he seemed puzzled. Confused.

"Please," Jane said, and her voice wasn't quite as demanding or as confident this time. Her hands shook, and her grip on the baseball bat was none too steady. "Please, take whatever you want. Just don't hurt my son."

"Hurt him?" he said, his voice barely more than a whisper. Tormented, pain-filled, and weak. "No, I could never… I love him. He's *my* son, my Benjamin, my…" Blinking as if to clear his eyes, he turned to stare at Cody's small, frightened face.

Jane lowered the bat, reached out a hand, flicked on the light switch. She saw the man jerk in shock, saw the fearful glance he sent up at the light fixture on the ceiling above him. Then his gaze returned to the top of Cody's head, because he held him too closely to see much else.

"He's my son," Jane said, calmly, gently, and her eyes were fixed to Cody's. The man was obviously insane. "His name is not Benjamin, it's Cody. He's my son. Please…"

The man gave his head a shake. With deliberate tenderness, he clasped Cody's small shoulders and moved the boy away from him, just a bit. Enough so that he could stare down into Cody's face.

"You're...you're not Benjamin...." he whispered, and the pain in his voice had tears springing to life in Jane's eyes.

"I'm Cody, mister. Cody Fortune. I had a dad once, but he died when I was a baby. That's my mom." Cody pointed. "Her name's Jane."

The man's brows rose. He shook his head slowly, and tears filled his eyes. "Lord," he whispered. "You're not... But...I thought..." Blinking repeatedly, he gripped the bedpost, pulled himself to his feet, but remained bent over, his free hand pressing to his forehead. Finally, he straightened, and turned to face Jane fully, right beneath the overhead light.

She saw his face, and her jaw fell. She caught her breath, forced her shock into submission. But then she noticed the clothes he wore, and her heart flip-flopped all over again.

Dear God, he was the image of the man in the painting.

"I'm sorry," he said, glancing down at Cody. Then facing Jane, he repeated, "I'm so sorry I frightened you both. I..." He took a step toward her, but swayed a little, and grasped the bedpost to hold himself up.

"Th-th-that's okay," Jane said, and she wiggled her hand at her son. Cody ran to her, and she held him tight, never taking her eyes off the stranger. "Um...look, how did you get in here?"

He frowned, and looked around the room as if for

the first time. "It's...it's different." He closed his eyes, pinched the bridge of his nose between thumb and forefinger.

Jane gently pushed Cody behind her, then took a backward step. She forcibly ignored his resemblance to the inventor she'd been mooning over so recently, and refused to think about his clothes. "You're, um...sick or something, aren't you," she said, almost as if to convince herself of it. "You're disoriented and you wandered in here by accident. I understand, all right? I'm not going to press charges, or anything like that."

The man's eyes opened. They were a bit dazed, clouded with pain, but they were also intelligent, perfectly sane and utterly sincere brown eyes. Brown eyes that looked so familiar it was downright uncanny. "What year is this, Jane?"

What year—

Jane swallowed hard and refused to so much as allow the thought to enter her mind. "Nineteen ninety-seven," she told him, as casually as if it were a question she answered every day. She nudged her son with her as she took another backward step into the hall.

The man's head jerked up fast and his eyes widened. "Nineteen..." Then he looked above him, at the light fixture in the ceiling, and when he lowered his head again, he grimaced in agony. "No... No, I went the wrong way. I came forward instead of going back. This can't be, I..." Still ranting, he lunged forward, toward Jane, but he never made it. He went down like a giant redwood, in a heap at her feet.

And that was when she noticed the gold wire-rims

on the floor beside him. The satchel in the middle of Cody's bedroom floor. The little black box. She swallowed hard and told herself she was letting her imagination run wild. She bent down over him, reached into his vest pocket and pulled out the pocket watch—the exact same pocket watch she'd seen in the painting. And then she looked more closely at the small black box on the floor. An odd-looking remote control that looked an awful lot like the box the inventor was tinkering with in the painting.

"He asked what year it was. Said he'd *come forward*," she muttered. And she mentally revisited what Sheriff O'Donnell, and the library books, had told her about the genius scientist who'd lived here. That he'd claimed to have invented time travel…and then he disappeared.

"But that just can't be…"

"Mom?"

She rose, and turned to face her son.

"Can we keep him?"

Jane braced her hands on the edge of the bed, bending almost double as she tried to catch her breath. The man was no lightweight, that was for sure. Getting him into the bed had been no easy job. And whoever he was, he could use a shower, a shave and a clean change of clothes.

None of which, she reminded herself, was her problem. All she had to do was go downstairs, call Sheriff Quigly O'Donnell and have this intruder taken away to a jail cell.

Except that she hadn't placed that call just yet. And she was in no hurry to, for some reason.

"Mom, is he sick?"

She glanced at her son, shrugged. "I don't know. Probably. You'd better go wash your hands, Cody. It might be catching."

Cody didn't go. "Maybe he's not sick, Mom. Maybe he's hurt."

Jane slipped her arm around her son's shoulders and squeezed. "You must have been scared to death."

"Nah. At first I thought he really was my dad. That he'd come back somehow—even though I know that's impossible. The way he was hugging me and all." His chin lowered just a bit. "It was kinda nice."

Jane's throat tightened. Time to change the subject. "How did he get in here, sweetheart?"

Cody shook his head. "There was this big light, right in the middle of my room. Round. Like…sort of like a train tunnel, only light instead of dark. Really light. It hurt my eyes." Jane frowned, but her son kept on talking. "Then the light was gone, and he was laying on the floor."

"Lying on the floor," she said automatically, her gaze pinned to the man in her son's bed.

"That's what I said. Mom, you think he's a *ghost?*"

"No, Cody, I don't think he's a ghost." She frowned at her son. "And I didn't think you believed in anything as non-scientific as that."

"I don't. But what about—?"

"Come on," she said, feeling uneasier by the second. A train tunnel, indeed. "Let's go call Sheriff O'Donnell."

"Mom, we *can't!*" Cody pulled his hand free. "He needs help! He's sick or hurt or something! You can't go putting him in jail!"

"Honey, he broke into our house—"

"He's my friend!" Cody crossed his arms over his chest, lower lip protruding.

"How can he be your friend? You don't even know him."

"He hugged me," Cody said firmly. "*And* he said he loved me. And I'm not going to let you put him in jail."

Jane closed her eyes and sighed. "Codester, sweetie, we can't just keep him."

"Why not? He could help with the tree house I want to build in the backyard. When he's better, I mean. It would be great. And we could—"

"For all we know, Cody, this man could be a dangerous criminal. We can't just let him stay. He could be—" She looked down into her son's huge green eyes and felt like Attila the Hun. "Cody..."

"Please, Mom? We at least have to find out who he is, where he came from. What that flash of light was all about. I think he needs help, Mom."

She sighed. "I'll think about it."

Cody smiled. Then he yawned and rubbed his eyes.

"Come on. You'd better get some sleep now. In my room, okay?"

"Okay." Grinning, Cody raced down the hall and shot right into her bedroom.

Jane looked at the man who slept in her son's bed. There was, of course, no way she was going to let him stay here. She'd simply have to wait until Cody went to sleep to call the sheriff. She'd figure out a way to explain it to him later. Meanwhile, she wouldn't take her eyes off the guy. If he so much as glanced in Cody's direction...

She picked up the baseball bat and pulled up a chair. She'd give Cody fifteen minutes to fall asleep. Then she'd place that call.

Zach awoke in the darkened room. His son's bedroom, of course. He must have tired himself out working today, and fallen asleep reading to the boy. It was a wonder Ben hadn't shaken him awake to get him to finish the story, the way he usually did.

But where on earth was Benjamin?

He closed his eyes, shook his head. Of course. Benjamin was still visiting his grandparents in Boston. How could he have forgotten?

Well, then, as long as he was awake, he might as well get some work done.

Oh, bother.

Zach poked into his shirt pocket in search of his spectacles, but didn't find them there. He reached to the small stand beside the bed for an oil lamp, but he must not have left it there. All he had to go by was the moonlight streaming in through the window behind him as he scanned the room in search of the lamp. But what was this? There was an incredibly beautiful young woman asleep in a wooden chair beside the bed. She wore a pale nightgown, with short sleeves that revealed her shapely arms. Her head was tipped sideways, resting upon her shoulder. And her hair rolled in waves of red-brown satin, halfway to the floor. My word, she was something. But what on earth was she doing here? How had she...

Slowly Zach recalled his colleagues Wilhelm and Eli, and their penchant for practical jokes. They'd been teasing him about working too hard, about having no life, no interests, aside from his son and his work. He'd once been something of a rogue, engaging in affairs with some of the town's most notoriously improper young women. But he'd been slacking off lately, and devoting all his time to the current experiment. One that would change the world, if he ever made it work.

Once, those two clowns had suggested he'd been so long without a woman that he wouldn't know what to do with one if she showed up in his bed. So they'd decided to hire some doxy to prove their point, had they? My, she was beautiful. Unfortunately, he wasn't so desperate to prove his manhood that he'd risk disease to do so. He much preferred to choose his own lovers. A shame, such a shame.

He sighed. No doubt she'd report back to those two childish pranksters that he'd failed to show any interest in her...charms.

Well, he could at least avoid the ribbing he'd take over that.

Sliding from the bed, wondering only briefly why he felt so weak and slightly dizzy, he tiptoed to the chair where she slept, nearly tripping over the baseball bat his son must have left lying about. Amazing he hadn't spotted it before. He shoved it out of the way with his foot and stepped closer to the trollop, and touched that long hair, rubbed it between his fingers. Soft as down. He bent slightly, inhaled her scent and smiled. Oh, they'd gone all out. Must have paid extra for a clean and lovely girl. This one looked as fresh as a daisy, and smelled even better.

As he stood bending over her, she sighed and moved a bit. Her lips parted and her head tipped back. And Zach realized with a pang how very long it had been since he'd kissed a woman. And, aside from the common cold, perhaps, he didn't fear catching anything by kissing this one.

So he did. He bent lower, lifted her chin with the tip of his forefinger and fit his mouth to hers. Her lips were warm and moist and pliant, and they felt good beneath his. Better when a gentle sigh escaped them, one he inhaled. He nudged those soft lips apart, to taste more of her, and they opened willingly, easily. She was starting to come awake now. Starting to respond, kissing him back. He slipped his arms around her small waist and pulled her to her feet, cradling her between his legs and against his chest as he deepened his kiss. Her drowsy response ignited feelings in him that he'd long since forgotten. Feelings he hadn't thought he'd ever know again. Passion flared in his veins, and her body pressed closer, head tilted farther, lips opened to his questing tongue. Her hands crept up his back, clung to his shoulders, and his heart beat a wild tattoo in his chest. No, none of his halfhearted dalliances had produced this strong a response in him.

Not since Claudia...

And then a mighty shove sent him staggering backward, and Zach was too surprised to even wonder why he was so weak that a mite of a woman could send him flying.

She stood panting, glaring at him. "That's it," she fairly growled at him. "That's it. I was thinking about going easy on you, mister, but you've pushed me too far."

"Rough or easy," he told her, "doesn't much matter. I'm not interested in having sex with you, Miss, so you might as well be on your way." It was a lie, of course. He was *very* interested. If only he had one of those condoms on hand, he might even oblige her.

"Not...interested... *Sex?*" She blinked as if in shock.

"Oh, it isn't you, love." He smiled at her, reached out a hand to smooth her hair out of her eyes. She only stood there, apparently too shocked to move. "Actually, I'm more tempted than I've been in a very long time. You're lovely. But I've no wish to expose myself to... Well, you understand."

She shook her head. "No. I don't understand, and I don't think I want to. Listen, you're nuts. You're certifiable. I'm taking you downstairs right now, and I'm calling the sheriff. But don't bother waiting around for him, okay? Just get out."

He frowned, tilted his head. "Pardon?"

"I said get out," she told him. She was grating her teeth and her fisted hands were shaking at her sides. "Get the hell out of my house. Now."

"My word," he told her. "You really should consider a career in the theater. I've no idea what you're up to, darling, but this is my house, and it's you who really ought to be leaving."

She blinked. The anger was rapidly fading. It was fear he saw replacing it in her eyes.

"I'm sorry," he said, thinking perhaps she'd be beaten if it became known she'd failed. He almost reconsidered his decision to abstain. Sex with this fiery woman would have to be something to experience. "What if I let you stay a couple of hours, hmm? Will that be enough to convince them we had ourselves a good tumble?"

Her hand connected with his face in a streak, and he didn't have time to duck it. It thoroughly amazed him when her blow knocked him off balance. He landed on the bed, blinking up at her. Lord, why was he so weak? So dizzy? Had he been ill recently?

"Get out," she ordered.

"Enough," he said softly, still baffled by his physical state. "Are you daft? Must I prove to you that this is my home? Shall I send for the sheriff to have you carried out? Is that what you want?" He shook his head, lifted a hand and pointed toward the table near the window, its shape just visible in the darkness. "There is a worktable. Not the main one, of course, but I do keep one here in Benjamin's room. Some of my experiments are there. My tools. My notes. They're secret, naturally, but a common doxy like you could make neither heads nor tails of them anyway, so go ahead and look." He pointed to the far wall. "There is the hearth, and upon the mantel are a pair of oil lamps and some matches. Do light one, so you can see for yourself where you are, woman. And then kindly remove yourself. I have work to do."

The woman only stared at him, completely puzzled. And then, slowly, she moved to the wall. She touched an appendage there, and the room was suddenly flooded with light. Zachariah Bolton nearly fell on the floor in shock.

Three

Jane searched the floor, spotted the baseball bat and snatched it up again as she watched an apparently bewildered man gazing around Cody's bedroom as if in disbelief.

"What is this?" he shouted. "Where is the slate board? My notes? Lord, woman, who installed this confounded electrical illuminator in here, and what have you done with my notes?"

"Look," she said, holding the bat up in front of her. "I don't know who the hell you are, or what you're talking about, but—"

"My tools!" he yelled, turning this way and that, pushing a hand through his nearly black hair. "What in tarnation have you done with my tools? And my worktable? Woman, where is Aunt Hattie's credenza?"

The man was sick. And not just mentally, either. His face was pale, and thinner than it should be, and dark circles ringed his deep brown eyes.

"Thank heavens," he said at last, and fell to his knees on the floor, grasping that small box. "The device is safe, at least. The device..." He looked even more confused than before. "But...but I hadn't finished it yet."

She wanted to run from the room. Right that sec-

ond, run down the hall to grab Cody, and then take
him right out of this house. But the man on his knees
in the center of the floor was looking at her, and she
thought, maybe, he was remembering... The pain
that slowly shadowed his face said more than words
could. But he spoke all the same, staring hard at her.

"You're Jane."

She nodded, not moving. Telling herself to leave,
call for help. And telling herself *not* to go to him and
try to ease the confusion from his brow.

"And the boy...he's your son... He's not Benjamin."

"That's right. You remember, then," she whispered.

He closed his eyes. "I remember. Benjamin...my
little Benjamin...he's..." His head bowed, and his
shoulders began to shake. "He's dying. How could
I forget that, even for a moment?"

Jane blinked. Dying? He had a son, who resembled
her own, and that son was dying? "My God," she
whispered, and the bat fell to the floor with a bang.
"My God, no wonder you're so messed up." Warily
she moved forward. And when she stood close to
where he knelt, she touched his hair, stroked it away
from his face and felt the tears that dampened it.

His arms closed around her legs, his head resting
against her thighs. "I meant to go back, Jane. I meant
to go back, so I could save him. Before he was ever
exposed to the blasted virus. I meant... But I failed.
A miscalculation. Something. I failed, and now I
might have lost him forever."

Crazy talk again. But then, how sane would she
be if she ever lost her Codester? A little chill raced

up her spine, but she went right on stroking his hair. His entire situation resembled the history of Zachariah Bolton. No wonder he'd wandered here in confusion. "It's all right," she whispered, because there was a lump in her throat that prevented her speaking louder. "It's going to be all right. I'll help you. Okay?"

He said nothing. But she knew he was devastated. He clung to her, shaking, crying perhaps, confused and in terrible pain.

"What's your name?" she asked him.

"Zach," he muttered. "Zachariah Bolton."

She stiffened, and he must have felt it, because he straightened away from her. He pressed a hand to his forehead, as if trying to rub away a pounding headache, and then he slowly got to his feet. "I'm sorry. I'm falling apart. What must you think?"

"I think," she said, choosing her words carefully, "that you've been through something horrible and it's left you...confused."

"Insane, you mean."

"Of course not."

He shook his head and paced away from her. "You look at me as if you believe I'm insane."

"I...well...look, it's just that Zachariah Bolton would be over a hundred and thirty years old today."

He stopped pacing and stood, toying with the black box in his hands. "Zachariah Bolton," he said softly, "is thirty-five years old, Jane. He was born in 1862."

"That doesn't make any— What is that thing you're playing with?"

He looked up, blinked. "So the house belongs to you now?"

"Yes. My son and I, yes."

"Your husband…is he at home? May I speak with him?"

"I don't have—" She bit her lip, averted her gaze. Since when did the handbook on survival in the nineties advise women to tell insane housebreakers that they were all alone? "He's not here right now."

The man who claimed to be Zachariah Bolton frowned, and his gaze shifted downward. To her left hand, she realized belatedly. "You're not married, are you?" She didn't answer. He shook his head in wonder, and looked down at the box in his hand once more. And then he swayed a little, blinked as if his vision were blurring.

"You're not well," she told him.

He drew a fortifying breath and eased himself down onto the edge of the bed. "No. No, physically, I'm not at all myself. Side effects, I suppose. I hadn't expected them to be quite so severe."

"S-side effects…to what?"

He looked her squarely in the eye. "You'll run off to send word to the local asylum if I tell you. But I don't suppose I have much of a choice right now, do I? I need you, Jane. I need you to… Ah, but I can't make you understand this way. Come here."

She blinked, took a step backward, eyeing him as he patted the spot on the bed beside him.

He frowned, and then his brows went up and he nodded. "Yes, I don't suppose I behaved as a gentleman when I found you here earlier, did I?" And his eyes, for some reason, fixed on her lips, and remained there a moment too long. "I don't know what that was, Jane. A memory lapse of some sort. Side effects, as I said. I was remembering a time when two of my colleagues hired a..." He gave his head a shake. "No matter. I apologize for that. Please, come over here, just for a moment. If you stand there, you might be hurt when I show you what this device does."

She tilted her head. "What is it, some kind of stun gun?"

His eyes narrowed. "I don't know that term, but no, that's not what this is. I only want to show you how I got here, Jane, because if I tell you, you'll think I'm insane and throw me out before I can offer proof."

She took a step toward him. He held out a hand. "I am Zachariah Bolton, Jane, and if you'll just come over here, I'll prove it."

Sighing, she picked up her baseball bat. He glanced down at it, lifting one eyebrow. Jane went to him, sat down beside him on the bed. "I suppose you're going to tell me you traveled a hundred years forward in time, and that this little remote control gone haywire is your time machine."

He frowned hard. "How on earth could you know—"

"Oh, everyone around here knows about Zachariah Bolton. He was a genius. A man light-years ahead of his time. But he got a little crazy after his..." Her voice trailed off, and she lost her breath.

"After his son died? Yes, I suppose I will go a bit crazy if that happens. But, Jane, I have no intention of letting it happen." Her eyes widened as she stared at him. He glanced down at himself. "I've been wearing these clothes all night, as I sat up with him. No wonder you were so afraid of me. I look like a common tramp. I hadn't expected anyone to be here...except for Ben and perhaps Mrs. Haversham."

She stood up, shook her head. "Stop. Just stop talking this way. It's..."

"Crazy?" He nodded. "I know. I know. That's what all my colleagues kept saying. That time travel was physically impossible. That I was wasting my talents working on it. I was close, oh, so very close, for months. When Benjamin took ill...it did something to me. Gave me something...extra."

She was still shaking her head, still backing away. But his hand came up and caught her wrist, holding her still, bringing her close to him. With the funny-looking remote, he pointed. "That spot, right there, Jane. A spot some thirty-five feet above the ground, a spot that this house ended up being built around... There's a wrinkle there. An invisible wrinkle in the fabric of time. A doorway, Jane. And I can open it."

His thumb touched a button on the remote, and she heard a low-pitched hum. A pinprick of light appeared in the air halfway between the floor and the ceiling, at the room's center.

"My intent was to go back, and only a few months. I wanted to go to my Benjamin before he'd ever been exposed to the virus, and take him away before he could become infected. I wanted to save him. Surely you can understand that, can't you, Jane? Only hours ago you were willing to face me down with nothing but a wooden bat in order to save your own child. You'd do anything for him. You know you would.''

She didn't like the way his eyes were blazing, or the tightness of his grip on her forearm. She pulled, but he got to his feet, gave one good tug, and she was pressed tight to him. His free arm snapped around her waist like a padlock's hasp, and he held her immobile. The fingers of his other hand worked the dial on the little black box, and the box began to hum. But the light remained the same.

"I messed it up, Jane," he said, his voice close to her ear, as he slowly turned a dial with his free hand. "My calculations were off somehow, and I came forward instead of going back. And not just a few months, but a century. A hundred years."

He gave the dial another twist, his grip on her waist tightening. She shook her head, but stopped pulling against his embrace. "This can't be," she whispered. "This just can't be."

Zach twisted the dial once more, but the light only flashed brighter for an instant and then died. For a long moment, Jane just stared at the spot where it had been.

He fiddled with the box, twisting the knob again, but nothing happened.

"Damn. I'm forgetting... I'm not insane," he whispered, and she realized, a little belatedly, that he was still holding her. Her back nestled intimately against the front of him, and his hand remained, lightly now, but snugly, at her waist. "The device needs time to recharge. How I let that slip my mind, I don't know. Three days, Jane, and I'll show you a wonder you'll never forget. I am exactly who I say

I am. I swear to you. And I need you, Jane. I need you to let me stay here until the device can recharge and I can get back to my son.''

She turned in his arms, stared up into his eyes and knew, without any doubt, that this man fully believed every word he was saying. This poor, beautiful, sick man.

"You won't turn me away. I know you won't. There's kindness in your eyes, Jane. I see it there. You won't—''

"You need help,'' she whispered. "Let me help you find it.''

He closed his eyes, his shoulders slumping forward as if he were too exhausted to go on. "At least,'' he whispered, "let me stay until morning. I'll think of a way to make you believe me by then. I'm too tired now. I can't think....''

"All right.'' Stupid, she told herself. Stupid to let an insane man stay the night. But she couldn't turn him away, not with that pain in his eyes. She just couldn't.

The relief in his face, in his eyes when he opened them again, was incredible. He pulled her closer, hugged her, rested his cheek in her hair. "Thank you, Jane,'' he told her. "Thank you.''

She was, he mused, perhaps the kindest woman he'd ever known. She'd suggested he get some rest, expressed concern over his health before she retired to her bed. Truth to tell, he was more than a bit concerned himself. That memory lapse...and this incessant weakness, and the recurring vertigo... Coming through the doorway had altered him physically, and he still wasn't certain of the extent of the damage. He'd fallen asleep instantly, and only awakened just now, to the sun rising high in the east. And he still felt exhausted and battered. His head ached intensely. But he had no time to waste lying in bed and waiting to recover. For all he knew, he might get worse, rather than better. Best, he decided, to get to work right away.

Work? But what work? What the hell could he do? Nothing, he realized slowly. Nothing but wait. He couldn't return to his own time until the device had recharged. So for three days he'd be here, unable to do a thing to help his son.

It wasn't hopeless. Merely a setback. He'd wait, and then he'd return. He'd return to the exact time whence he'd come. Benjamin's condition would not have had time to worsen. And from there, Zach would simply start over. Make a few adjustments, and try again. In the meantime, there was very little he could do. His main task, it seemed, was proving himself to Jane, convincing her to let him remain right here, for there was no other place....

Yes. He'd have to convince Jane to let him stay. Fortunately, Zach thought, influencing reluctant females to his way of thinking was one of his areas of expertise. Second only to science, in fact. Or had been, once. He wondered briefly whether he could drum up enough of his legendary charm to sway her. He had to try. There was more at stake than conquest here. There was Ben. Benjamin was safe...for the moment. So Zach was free to pursue the matter at hand.

But first...

He glanced down at his rumpled clothing and wrinkled his nose. First a bath, and a change of clothes. His carpetbag still lay on the floor, where he'd dropped it when he first came through. So at least he had the most recent notes—torn hastily from his journal in case he might need them—a few basic tools, a change of clothes and some toiletries. He carried these with him into the bathroom down the hall, and then marveled at the wonders to be found there.

At first he wondered how he'd manage without a lamp or a candle. But then he recalled the electric illuminator in Benjamin's—er, Cody's—room, and searched the spot on the wall just inside the door, where the control for the other one had been. He found the switch, moved it, and the bathroom filled with light. Zach simply shook his head in wonder, and explored further. The tub was huge, with spigots fixed into it. Water, hot, as well as cold, ran into the giant shining tub at the touch of a knob. Far more advanced than his own bathroom had been, and his had been the very latest in technology. Judging by the force with which the water spewed from the spigots, he knew there must be more power behind it than mere gravity. The necessary, too, was sparkling-clean and water-filled. Warm air blew gently from a register low on the wall. He smelled no wood smoke. Something else was obviously heating the water, and the house, as well. The very essence of day-to-day living, he realized slowly, had changed. Drastically changed.

He ran water into the tub, and soaked for a long time as he tried to imagine what other advances he'd discover in this new era. Automobiles… Had they proved practical, or been a passing fancy, as so many of his colleagues had predicted? Had this new generation of humanity wiped out disease? Achieved world peace? And this woman, Jane, owning this house filled with modern wonders and raising a son all on her own. Was this common today? Zach frowned as he considered it. Something told him that nothing about Jane was common.

He'd kissed her. Yes, he'd been in the throes of some sort of delirium when he did it, but not so much so that he couldn't recall every instant of that kiss. And her sleepy response to it. Her soft breath in his mouth, her hands splayed on his shoulders. She'd set a fire in him that he hadn't felt in a very long time. Perhaps ever. Oh, there'd been passion between him and Claudia, one he suspected was based more on his own youth and energy than anything else. But they'd really had very little in common. And, of course, he'd learned later that he'd been no more than an amusing diversion to her. She hadn't cared for him in the least. He'd been young, with little money and few prospects. She'd been married to a wealthy man, a woman of social standing who couldn't risk it all by admitting to her frequent affairs with naive young men. Much less admitting that she had become pregnant as a result of one of them.

She'd gone abroad to visit an aunt, or so the story went. Months later, Benjamin had been dropped upon Zachariah's doorstep, with a note promising Zach he'd be ruined, both socially and financially, if he ever breathed a word about the child's mother.

She'd never wanted to lay eyes on the baby or on his father again.

And so she never had.

It had been, Zach mused, the best education he could ever have. Oh, he'd learned all about women. They were practical creatures. No woman would be truly interested in a man who was less than wealthy—particularly if he was less wealthy than she. Claudia's interest had recently been renewed. No doubt due to the fact that her rich husband had passed, leaving most of his money to a nephew. And in the years in between, Zach had acquired his own wealth and social standing. But he was no longer interested in Claudia. For a time he'd become a user of women, the way he'd once been used by one of them. Once he understood how the game was played, he'd suffered no further delusions about romance or love.

Perhaps the lovely Jane had learned the lesson, as well, in a manner much the same as he'd learned it himself. Or perhaps she was simply a lonely widow. Though most widows of Zach's acquaintance continued to wear their wedding bands. That gave him pause.

Jane. Beautiful, brave, passionate Jane. She looked like an angel. But she kissed like a woman too long without a man. He could, he mused, take care of that problem for her. His thoughts surprised him, since he'd given up his roguish ways long ago. But then, he'd been very long without a woman's touch, and hers had been...incredible. He had three days here, after all, and little else to do besides wait.

Oh, yes. And a well-planned seduction would

probably go a long way in helping to convince the little skeptic that he was who he said he was. Or at least convincing her to let him stay.

He swallowed hard at the thoughts racing through his mind. Was it some added side effect of the time travel making him addle-brained, or was it *her?* Either way, it didn't matter. He thought he had come up with a far simpler means to convince her now.

As he soaked, there was a knock at the door, followed by Jane's voice. "Are you decent?"

Some devil came to life inside him, all over again, and it was that devil who made him call, "Come in." Perhaps he was testing her to judge her reactions, so that he might gauge what sort of woman he was dealing with. A test, much like the many other experiments he'd performed in his day. He ignored the tiny voice in his brain that told him that theory was nothing more than self-deception. The woman got to him, in a way that disturbed him far too much to admit, even to himself.

The bathroom door opened, and the woman he'd been thinking about stepped inside. Aside from an initial start of surprise, she showed no reaction at all. Keeping her eyes averted, she moved through the room, extracting big, emerald green towels from a cabinet, and then a small pink plastic item, and a can of some sort. "If you were trying to shock me, you chose the wrong method," she said. "I was raised with brothers." She set the towels and the other items on a shelf beside the tub, and still without looking at him, turned to go.

"Jane?" She stopped, her back to him. She wore a robe now, over the thin nightgown of the night before. Pity. But that glorious hair still hung loosely down her back, making him ache to run his hands through it once again. "What is this?" he asked.

"I thought you'd want to shave." She still didn't turn.

Frowning, Zach leaned forward and picked up the pink thing, turning it this way and that. "This bit of a thing is a razor?" He could clearly see, upon closer inspection, that that was precisely what it was.

"Of course it is."

He sighed loudly, and achieved the desired results. She turned, but kept her eyes carefully glued to his face. "Could you...could you show me how it works, Jane? They've changed drastically in the past hundred years."

Her eyes narrowed as they searched his, and he tried desperately to keep the mischief hidden. He started to get up. "Stay where you are," she told him.

"I'll need a mirror—"

"Not if I'm doing the shaving," she said. Then she knelt beside the tub, picked up one of the towels and handed it to him. "Cover your—yourself," she told him.

"And soak this wonderful towel?"

Frowning at him, Jane dropped the towel into the water, so that it landed right in his lap, no doubt concealing the parts of his anatomy she'd rather not be tempted to look at too closely. Then she took up the can, shook it and depressed a button on its top. Mounds of white foam oozed from the spout and into her palm. Zach felt his eyes widen. Then she leaned over and smoothed the lotion onto his face. Her touch was warm, and trembling, and so good that he closed his eyes and relished it.

When she finished, she dipped her hands into the water to rinse them clean. Her fingertips brushed his thigh, and he knew then that certain bodily functions had not been damaged by the side effects of time travel. He hoped she didn't notice the change in the shape concealed by that towel.

"Now, you just take the razor and..." She demonstrated, by drawing the blade very carefully down over his cheek. "Just like that. You see?"

"Mmm..." he said. Then he opened his eyes and saw her scowling at him. "I mean, yes, of course. But...suppose I cut myself?"

"If you are who you say you are, then you've managed a straight edge in your time. And if you can handle that, you can handle this." She set the razor on the edge of the tub and got up to leave.

"I am who I say I am, Jane. And you'll believe it before breakfast. I promise."

She looked at him for a long moment, and this time her eyes betrayed her, dipping down to gaze at his chest and belly. Hastily she turned and left the room, closing the door firmly behind her.

Jane leaned back against the bathroom door and tried to steady her breathing. Whoever he was, the lunatic in her bathtub was incredible. And that made him dangerous. The sooner he was out of her house, the better. She closed her eyes, but still the image of that muscled chest, beaded with water, kept resurfacing in her mind. "The sooner the better," she muttered, and headed downstairs to start breakfast.

When she had the coffee brewing and Cody's favorite blueberry muffins in the oven, Jane went upstairs again to wake her son. But Cody was no longer in bed when she stepped into her room. For just a second, his absence startled her. And then she heard the reassuring sounds of his Nintendo game from down the hall, and sighed. As she dressed, she glanced up at the painting that hung on the wall above her bed...and then she went still, falling into the brown eyes of the man in that painting. The inventor. The time traveler.

He'd hopped right out of a Jules Verne novel and landed smack in the middle of her life.

Or so the man who'd somehow become her houseguest would have her believe. It was, to say the least, mind-boggling. The coincidence of it, anyway. He looked so much like the man in the painting. Even his clothes...

But it was impossible, of course. Still, something about the man pulled at her. She wanted to help him. And today she would. She'd convince him to let her take him into town, to see a doctor. Maybe he'd taken a blow to the head or something.

She hadn't warned Zach not to tell Cody where he thought he'd really come from, or who he thought he really was, and she should have. Lord, she could just imagine the call she'd get when Cody started sharing that tale with his fifth-grade class next week at school. Besides, it would only confuse him. He was far too young to grasp a concept like that, despite his above-average intelligence.

She finished dressing and went down the hall, then stood in Cody's doorway and stared for a moment.

Cody stood near the desk, laughing uproariously as the man who claimed to be Zachariah Bolton, genius, worked the control pad, unerringly marching the little Mario on the screen right off a cliff and into oblivion.

He made an aggravated sound in his throat.

"Don't feel bad," Jane said. "I've been trying for months, and I still can't get past World Two."

Both of them turned to face her, and both were smiling. Zach's eyes glittered with something like wonder. "This," he said softly, "is amazing."

"And addictive. Be careful, or you'll find yourself glued to that thing like a fly in a spider's web." His smile broadened and she caught her breath. Clean and shaved, he was even more breathtaking. Especially when he smiled. Her errant mind chose that moment to recall the way that smiling mouth had felt when it made love to hers last night, and she quickly averted her eyes. Too late, though. He'd seen it. She saw the way his gaze lowered to her lips for just an instant. And she felt the air between them change.

She cleared her throat. "And, Cody, what have I told you about Nintendo before breakfast?"

"I know, Mom. But Zach's never seen anything like this. Have you, Zach?"

"Certainly not."

"Heck, Mom, they didn't even have TV in 1897."

She grimaced and shot a glance at him. "You didn't tell him—"

"He figured it out all by himself, Jane. Of course, it took him several guesses. As I recall, the first one was that I was a traveler from another planet. And then that I was a ghost. And finally that I was a…" He frowned. "What did you call it, Cody?"

"A time cop," Cody said.

Jane sighed. "I knew I never should have let you rent that Van Damme movie."

"Jane, really," Zach said. "Your language."

Jane rolled her eyes. "Breakfast will be ready in fifteen minutes," she told them both. "Be there."

"We will, Mom."

She eyed them both, wondering whether it was truly safe to leave Cody alone with the man, as delusional as he was.

"Don't go just yet, Jane," the man said, and he set the control pad down and got to his feet. "I have something to show you. In my satchel." He went to the bed, where the bag rested, unbuckled it and reached inside. What he pulled out was a newspaper, and he turned to face her, holding it out. "I promised I'd prove myself to you before breakfast. Go on, take it."

Swallowing hard, Jane stepped forward and took the crisp newspaper. It was so new she could still smell the ink. The *Rockwell Sentinel,* it said across the front—31 August 1897.

She blinked and looked up at him. Cody had forgotten all about his game, and was standing close beside her. "Wow. It's really true," he said in awe.

"Cody, these things can be made to order. You know that." Her eyes met Zach's. "I'm sorry, but this isn't good enough."

"I was afraid it might not be. Fortunately, I have more." He came closer to her, took her arm and turned her slightly, pointing. "There is a loose floorboard, the fourth one from that wall," he told her, pointing as he did. "Beneath it is my journal. Records I kept of the work I was doing. I put them there for safekeeping out of habit. My field is wrought with competitors, not all of them honest men. The notes are there, with the exception of one page. One I tore out and brought with me. Notes and figures I would need should the device require adjusting or repair.''

She stared at him, then at the floor, where he was pointing.

"Come, let's look. We need to get your skepticism out of the way, if I'm going to be able to proceed.''

"Look, Mom,'' Cody begged. "He's telling the truth, I know he is!''

Shrugging, Jane moved to the spot he'd indicated. She bent down, pressing on the loose board with her hands, gasping and drawing away when it moved. She glanced his way, licking her lips, and then attempted to pull the board up.

"Allow me.'' He bent down beside her and pulled the loose end of the board until it came up a few inches. He held it there while she thrust her hands beneath and pulled out a heavy leather-bound journal. Then she sat down on the floor, pulling it into her lap.

"I can't believe...''

"You must believe, Jane. Please, open it up. Look at it.''

She brushed the dust from the leather cover and opened the book. The pages had yellowed and curled with time. But the handwriting on them was still legible. She shook her head in wonder.

"Several pages in, find the place where a page is missing.''

Nodding quickly, Jane turned the pages, taking

care with them due to their fragile condition. She found the spot where jagged, yellowed edges were all that remained, and looked up into his eyes. He pulled a folded page from his vest pocket, smoothed the sheet and handed it to her. It was white and crisp and new. She took the page from him, stared at it in wonder, and then laid its uneven edge against the jagged, yellowed place in the book.

And the edges lined up perfectly. She scanned the pages, and noticed that the handwriting was identical, as well.

"My God," she whispered. "My God, it's true."

Her hands, still holding the page, began to tremble.

"I'm sorry to shock you this way," he told her gently. "But, Jane, I must convince you to let me stay here. Work here, until I can find out what went wrong with the experiment. I have to go back."

Her head came up, her eyes meeting his. "To save your son."

"Yes. Yes, I must prevent him from dying. If I can go back, return to a time before Benjamin was exposed, I can take him away. He'll never become sick, never die. And, Jane, I must do it from here, from this very room."

"Why?" she asked him, and she slowly realized that she was believing this man. In shock over what he was claiming, but still *believing* it.

"There's something here, some force, some sort of wrinkle in the fabric of time, as I told you before. My device opens a doorway into that void, and allows me to travel through it. But I've attempted opening the doorway in other areas, outdoors, on the ground, in other rooms. It doesn't function, Jane. Only here. Only in this very room.''

He sighed and lowered his head. ''And I must admit, there's a distinct possibility that the doorway is limited. That my travel will only take me from this time to my own, and back again. I might return only to experience the death of my son, and be unable to stop it.''

He seemed surprised when he looked down to see Jane blinking tears from her eyes. ''I don't know what I would do if I lost Cody,'' she told him. ''It would kill me, I think.''

''Then you understand how important this is to me.''

She nodded. ''Of course I understand. I'm a mother. How could I not?''

''Then…''

Jane licked her lips, drew a fortifying breath, and then saw the plea in Cody's eyes, identical to the one in Zach's. ''All right,'' she said at last. ''All right, you can stay. For as long as you need to.''

He sighed, every muscle in his body relaxing at once, as the tension was visibly washed away.

''Thank you. It isn't enough, I know, but…'' He shook his head, as if words failed him. ''Thank you.''

Jane got to her feet, pressed his journal into his hands. ''I just hope you can do this—go back far enough, I mean.''

He closed his eyes as the agony of possible failure washed over him, nearly buckling his knees. ''I have to.''

"Maybe not," Cody said quickly. "What was it that killed your son, Zach?"

He sighed hard. "Quinaria fever," he said softly.

Cody grinned, but Jane's heart almost stopped beating. She'd forgotten. My God, how had she forgotten? She gripped Cody's arm to stop him. "Cody, no—"

"We can cure that now," he said. "You don't have to worry about trying to go back to a time before Benjamin got sick. All we have to do is get the medicine for you, Zach, and you'll be able to make him well again."

He stared at Cody, gaping. And then he grabbed Jane's son, and hugged him tightly to his chest.

Jane stood there, watching them, trying to breathe, though her chest felt tight and heavy. She knew that she couldn't let this happen. She had to stop Zach from saving his beautiful, sick little boy.

Because if he did, there was a good chance she'd end up losing her own.

Four

She left them. There was nothing she could do. Not now, not with Cody standing there listening to every word. She had three days. Three days to find a way to keep Zachariah Bolton from returning to the past and curing his dying child.

My God, she must be some kind of monster to be thinking this way! How could she? But Cody... Cody was everything to her. All she had, all she'd ever wanted. If she lost him...

She knuckled a tear from her eye and told herself she was right. Benjamin's death had saved countless lives. It was meant to be, and as painful as that knowledge was, it was there. It was meant to be. You couldn't just go around altering history.

She bit her trembling lip. Maybe there was another way....

Damn, she'd drive herself crazy thinking about this. It made her dizzy when she considered the magnitude of it all, the ramifications, the impossibility of it. She deliberately focused on taking the blueberry muffins from the oven, setting the table. She had time. Three days. For now, she just needed to get through breakfast.

Cody and Zach showed up in the kitchen a short time later, and Jane was relieved to see that Cody had showered and dressed. She served up blueberry muffins and scrambled eggs, and as she shook out Cody's daily vitamin tablet she decided Zach could use one as well.

He took the little pill from her hand and eyed it.

"You're still not looking all that great," she told him. "It's a vitamin supplement. It's good for you." He shrugged and swallowed the tablet, washing it down with his orange juice. The entire time he ate, Jane noticed his curious gaze darting around the kitchen, at the appliances, the light fixtures, the microwave. He was brimming with questions, she knew he was. But he also kept looking at her, and though she tried to hide the worry, she knew it must show in her eyes. Because his were probing and questioning. She avoided that disturbing gaze of his, bustling around the kitchen, getting butter for the muffins and refilling coffee cups and juice glasses before they were half-empty.

"Jane," he said, when she finally ran out of things to do, and sat down to eat. "Is something wrong? Have you had second thoughts about letting me stay?"

And then a car pulled into the drive, stopping near the shop, and saving her from having to answer. She couldn't tell him. Not yet. She wasn't even sure how to tell him, and she certainly couldn't do it in front of Cody. She needed to speak to him when they were alone together, and only after she'd found the right words to convince him to give up this insane quest.

"I have to..." she began, but her words trailed off, because Zach was on his feet, rushing to the door, gazing out at the car with amazement on his face.

Jane couldn't stop herself from smiling as she walked up behind him. "It's a car. Um…an automobile. They…" The horn sounded. "Gee, Zach, I have an impatient customer to tend to. The explanation is going to have to wait until later."

"Go on, Mom. Me and Zach'll be fine." Cody came to stand close to Zach's other side.

"Zach and I," Jane said. "A whiz kid is supposed to know grammar."

Cody made a face at her, then glanced up at Zach. "You've seen cars before, right, Zach?"

Zach nodded, his gaze remaining riveted to the late-model Cadillac out front. "Nothing like that one, my boy."

Jane sighed. There wasn't any time to lose. She moved past them, out the door and down the driveway to the little shop resting at the end. And she knew as soon as she saw the car's passenger that she was in for a long visit. Isabelle Curry, the town of Rockwell's librarian and resident gossip. Fortunately, she was also an avid antique collector. A good customer, but a trying one. "Give me strength," Jane muttered, and plastered a smile on her face.

"Amazing," Zach said, trailing his hand over the smooth, gleaming red finish of the automobile, peering through the windscreen. "The glass is darkened."

"To keep the sun outta your eyes," Cody explained. "Why don't you get inside it, Zach? Mrs. Curry won't mind. She's nice."

"I don't think..." Zach stopped speaking when Cody pulled the door open, giving him a better view inside the machine. He couldn't stop himself. He poked his head into the thing and ran his hand over the soft plush fabric of the seats. And then he jumped a bit, because the boy had opened the door on the other side and jumped into the car.

"C'mon, Zach. I'll show you how it works."

"Cody, that probably isn't—"

"Look," Cody said, pointing. "It has a radio, and a CD player, so you can listen to music while you drive."

Cody twisted a set of keys that were dangling from the steering wheel, and then punched a button. Loud music—or something that vaguely resembled music—flooded the vehicle.

Amazed, Zach slid inside, settling himself behind the wheel and ignoring the deafening sounds.

"It's really easy to drive it," Cody said loudly. "Even I know how."

"You?"

"Sure. I watch Mom all the time."

"Your *mother* owns an automobile?"

"Sure she does. How do you think we go any-place? It's in the garage, over there." He pointed, and Zach noticed the small outbuilding near where the pony shed used to be. "Look, it's simple," Cody went on. "First, you turn the key, like this..."

Cody turned the key still farther, and the vehicle came to life. Zach felt a smile splitting his face as the vibration of the motor moved through him, smooth and efficient and quiet. Far removed from the autos he'd driven.

"Then you just move this shift, here," Cody went on, as if thrilled with his role as teacher. "Push that pedal to go, and the other one to stop. Simple."

"There's no choke? No clutch?"

"Nope." Cody's eyes had taken on a decidedly mischievous gleam. "Wanna try it?"

Zach chewed his lip, truly torn. On the one hand, this was not his machine, and he had no business experimenting with it. On the other…oh, the wonder of it! He could barely contain the excitement coursing through him.

The decision was taken from his hands a second later, when Cody yanked on the shifting lever and the auto lurched backward. Its hindquarters were pointed directly toward the guest house at the end of the drive, and Zach barely managed to turn the wheel and alter its direction in time to miss the building. He stomped on the pedal that he thought was supposed to stop the thing, but instead it went faster.

"Tarnation!" he exclaimed, steering madly as the auto raced backward in a loopy pattern across the lawn.

"I shifted wrong!" Cody shouted, and yanked on the lever yet again. There was a horrible grinding sound. The vehicle lurched and bucked, suddenly changing direction and heading forward now.

Jane and a heavyset, bejeweled woman had emerged from the guest house. Both waved their arms and shouted, though Zach couldn't hear what they said, with the music blasting in his ears and Cody's uproarious laughter. The auto bounded over the grass, across the drive, and pointed its beak right at the two women. They split as it rolled between them. Zach glanced over his shoulder to see the older woman picking herself up off the ground. If her face was any indication, she was hopping mad.

He tried the other pedal, and the vehicle ground to a stop so suddenly that he had to grab hold of the boy to keep him from being flung forward and hitting his head. He didn't dare remove his foot from the pedal. Though when the two women came running toward him, he was tempted to do just that. Free up his feet for a quick escape.

Jane got to the vehicle first, yanked the door open and reached past him to move the lever once more. With a snap of her wrist, she twisted the keys and yanked them out of the car when the motor died.

"What in the name of God do you think you're doing?" she screamed at Zach. Then her face softened as she sought the eyes of her son. "Cody, sweetheart, are you okay?"

"Sure, Mom. I was just showing Zach how to drive, is all." He slanted a glance at Zach. "He's not very good at it, though, is he?"

The other woman had arrived now, spluttering and red-faced. "Who is this person, and what in the world is he doing in my car?"

"It's all right, Mrs. Curry," Jane said soothingly, turning to the woman. "No harm done. The car is fine, see?"

Cody got out his side, and Zach figured it would be a good idea to do the same. He was embarrassed beyond measure.

"It was my fault," Cody said, hurrying around the car. "I wanted to try driving your car, Mrs. Curry. I thought I knew how. Gee, if Zach hadn't jumped in and stopped it, I don't know what I would have done.''

Jane's eyes widened to the size of saucers, and she glared at her son. ''Cody Nicholas Fortune, you know better than to—''

''Oh, my!'' said Mrs. Curry, rushing to Cody and hugging him against her ample belly until Zach wondered if the boy would be smothered. ''You poor child. You must have been so frightened. Oh, Jane, you mustn't punish him for this. Boys will be boys, you know. I never should have left the keys in the ignition with a child of his age nearby. Whatever could I have been thinking?''

She released Cody, who sent his mother an angelic smile. And then Zach found himself embraced by the ubiquitous Mrs. Curry. ''And you!'' she ranted, squeezing him until his seams nearly popped. ''A true hero. Chasing down that car and jumping in to save a little boy! What courage!''

''Thank you,'' he managed, but his words were muffled by her embrace.

She released him, beaming. ''Jane, dear, aren't you going to introduce me to this modern-day superman?''

Jane—from behind gritted teeth, Zach suspected—said, ''Of course. Isabelle Curry, meet Zachariah B—'' She bit her lip.

''Bolton,'' Zach finished automatically. Jane made her eyes huge and sent him a look that would wilt fresh lettuce. ''Er…the third,'' he added.

Isabelle blinked. ''Of course! I would know you anywhere. My goodness, have you any idea how much you resemble your grandfather?''

"I've been told it's quite remarkable," Zach said.

"I should say so. Whatever brings you to Rockwell, Mr. Bolton?"

Zach frowned and searched his brain.

"He's, er...tracing his family tree," Jane said quickly.

"Yes. I was very eager to see what my... grandfather's house looked like today."

"Well, of course you are," Isabelle said. "Where are you staying while you're here, Zachariah?"

"Here," he said.

Jane's eyes burned holes through him.

"Here?" Isabelle repeated. Her excitement died a slow death, and something else replaced it in her eyes as she looked from him to Jane and back again. "With Jane?"

Jane lowered her forehead into her palm.

"Well, now, isn't that...nice?" Isabelle said. She turned to Jane, but when their eyes met, the smile left Isabelle's lips. "I really should be on my way. Lots to do, you know." She held out a hand to Jane. "My keys, dear."

Jane handed them over, then looked on as Isabelle got into the car and started the engine. The woman grimaced when the music blasted, and poked her thumb on a button a little harder than was probably necessary to shut the sound off. A second later, she was gone, spewing gravel in her wake.

Jane pushed her hair back with both hands, tipping her head skyward. "I don't even know where to begin."

"I apologize, Jane," Zach said. "I was so intrigued by the automobile that I used poor judgment.''

"You," she said, poking him in the center of his chest with her finger, "are not to get anywhere near a car again unless I'm with you. Got it?''

He nodded, but couldn't help smiling a bit at her anger.

"And *you*," she said to her son. "You lied to Mrs. Curry. How many times have I told you about honesty?''

"Well, gee, Mom, I couldn't tell her the truth. That Zach didn't know how to drive because he came from another time, and stuff. She wouldn't have believed me.''

"You...you..." Jane looked helplessly at Zach. Zach shrugged.

"Besides, you lied to her, too.''

"Well, yes, but..." She blinked slowly. "Cody, I..." And finally shook her head. "You're right. I lied, too, and it was wrong. Unfortunately, I had to.''

"So instead of never telling lies at all, we should never tell lies unless we have to?" Cody asked innocently.

The child's intelligence was astounding. And Zach knew the boy was only teasing his mother at this point. Fortunately, Jane knew it, too. He could tell by the narrowing of her eyes. She dropped down to her knees and took her son by the shoulders. "There might be times, Cody, when you have to tell a lie to other people, especially if you're doing it to avoid hurting someone or causing a whole lot of trouble, or because you know you won't be believed anyway. But there will never, never, be a time when you will have to lie to me. Understand? No matter what you have to tell me, Codester, I'll believe you. So you'll never have to keep the truth from me. All right?''

Cody smiled. "Okay, Mom."

"Good."

"Can I go ride my bike now?"

She nodded, and he turned and raced away toward the back of the house.

Zach couldn't take his eyes from her.

"What are you looking at?" she asked when she met his gaze at last.

He shook his head slowly. "I..." He cleared his throat. "Your son is very lucky to have you for a mother, Jane Fortune."

A pink blush crept up her neck and spread into her face. Zach resisted the urge to reach out with his hand, and feel the warmth of it.

She blinked, perhaps in confusion. "Compliments aren't going to get you out of this, Zachariah. You screwed up."

"Mrs. Curry will get over it."

"Sure she will, but not before she's told everyone in town that I'm a shameless hussy who's captured herself one hell of a hunk and is parading him around right in front of her impressionable son."

"What," he asked, "is a hunk?"

Her blush deepened and she lifted her brows. "I didn't say hunk, I said skunk."

"I distinctly heard you say hunk."

"My reputation is ruined. They'll probably report me as an unfit mother."

"You think Mrs. Curry believes we're...er..."

"Having sex?" she inserted, and Zach blinked at

her casual use of the words. "Of course she does. What else would she think?"

"I fail to see why she'd jump to such a drastic conclusion."

"Take a look in the mirror, Zach. Mrs. Curry isn't numb from the neck down, or blind, or gay. And she's probably pretty sure I'm not any of those things, either." She shook her head. "Lord, I hope it doesn't make the *Rockwell Daily Star.* 'Local Spinster Living in Sin. Read all about it!'"

Zach resisted the urge to laugh. She was sincerely upset over the blemish he'd caused to her reputation. Though it was difficult to focus on that, when he was fairly certain she'd just said she found him attractive. Unless he'd misunderstood.

"Gossip hasn't changed much, has it?"

"Nothing's changed in this little town, Zach. Anywhere else, it wouldn't matter if I paraded men in and out of my bedroom day and night. No one would care. Here, though, we have Isabelle Curry, Rockwell's answer to modern morality, and her partner in crime, Pastor McDermott. And they're both on the school board, too." She shook her head.

"I'm sorry," Zach told her, and he meant it. "Perhaps we could say I was renting a room from you, or…"

"No one would believe it, Zach."

Zach sighed, truly sorry for causing Jane so much strife. "I suppose the best thing I can do is get hold of that miracle drug of yours as soon as possible, and be on my way. Surely your reputation can survive a mere three days of living in sin?" She rolled her eyes. "Meanwhile, Jane, would it be better if I were to stay here in the guest house?"

"It's not a guest house anymore."

Zach looked past her, at the guest house—or at what had been the guest house. Now bric-a-brac lined shelves beyond the windows, and a sign above the door read Times Remembered—Fine Antiques and Collectibles.

"Would you like to see it?" she asked softly. And though he really should have been beginning the search for this new drug, Zach found himself nodding. A few more minutes wouldn't matter.

"Yes," he said. "I'd like that very much."

The smile that touched her lips, and the light in her eyes, told Zach that this little enterprise meant something to her. And that she was proud of it. She led him through the front doors, and Zach didn't recognize the place. The entire building had been converted, partitions knocked down. It was one large room now, with a long counter across the back side, and rows of shelves everywhere else. The shelves were lined with too many items to name. Canisters, dishes, knickknacks, music boxes. There was an entire section of books, another with artwork. And a large corner had been left open, for several pieces of furniture that had been cleaned and polished until they shone. An oak rocking chair. A sewing machine. A pedestal table.

Each item in the shop had a price tag dangling from it. And on the counter in the back sat a large black cash register that had obviously come from his time, as well. Zach doubted he'd recognize its modern-day counterpart.

"I'm impressed, to say the least, Jane. A woman setting up and running her own business. Owning her own home and automobile. Raising her son alone."

She waved a dismissive hand at him. "Don't be impressed until I make enough money to expand."

"Are you...having financial problems, then?"

She smiled at him. "Zach, my family is one of the wealthiest in the country. I have trust funds and interest-bearing accounts enough to buy the moon."

Zach tilted his head. "I don't understand. Why—"

"Growing up in Minneapolis, I lived in my father's mansion. Servants at my beck and call. More clothes than I could wear in a year. Cars and private schools and money, money, money."

"And?"

"And I hated it. Zach, Fortune Cosmetics is a monster. My family think they're running the business, but the truth is, it's running them. My father is so jealous of my uncle Jake that they can barely speak without an argument. And they're brothers. My mother...all she cares about is money and scheming to get more of it. I just didn't want any part of that. Not for me, and especially not for Cody."

She shrugged and paced toward him, eyes dreamily scanning the aisles of her shop. "I've always been the old-fashioned one. My grandmother...she knew that about me. More than I ever realized. When she died, she left me this place. So I left home to come out here and try to find a simpler life." She looked up at him, and smiled fully. "And instead, I got a time-traveling inventor."

"Not exactly simple," Zach said. "I find it amusing, Jane, that you see yourself as an old-fashioned woman. To me you seem the opposite. Strong. Independent. A freethinker. Everything I always…'' he stopped himself from finishing when he realized he was going to say ''wanted.'' ''Everything I always thought of as modern,'' he said instead. It was true, what he'd been thinking, he confirmed, a bit surprised. Oh, yes, he'd had his share of women since Claudia had broken his naive young heart. But all the while, he'd scoffed at their docile ways and insipid giggles. Their meek manners and false shyness. Their constant quest for wealthy husbands. Deep inside, he'd secretly wished for a modern woman. One who had her own opinions and lived as no man's servant. Not a fainting, timid, helpless child, but a woman like…a woman like Jane Fortune.

Not that he wanted any woman bound to him. Not even one like this. No, he'd learned his lessons too well for that. But just to know one. Just to be with her…

''Maybe I'm modern from a nineteenth-century point of view, Zach,'' she said. ''But to a twentieth-century mind, I'm the one stuck in a time warp.''

Zach drew in a breath, let it out slowly. ''Tell me about…about Cody's father.''

Jane's head came up quickly, her soft brows bending together. ''No.''

''I didn't mean to pry, Jane. I was just wondering how such an old-fashioned girl managed to—''

''I really should be working on the books,'' she told him. ''Why don't you go back to the house and finish your breakfast?''

He'd touched on a tender subject, then. All right.

He told himself he wouldn't ask again. Though, for some reason, he was dying to know about the man who'd fathered Jane Fortune's child.

"Yes, I suppose I will," he said. And he managed to take his eyes off her, turn and leave the shop.

"We have lunch at noon," she told him as he started through the door.

He nodded, and closed it behind him.

Jane had more customers that morning than she'd had since she'd opened the shop. A few of them even bought something. The rest, she was convinced, had come to see if they could catch a glimpse of the man Isabelle Curry had no doubt told them about. The man who was living in sin with an unmarried mother. Damn. It had been hard enough seeing the speculation in their eyes when she arrived here. Everyone wanted to know where her husband was. Most came right out and asked, though a few were subtler. She didn't blame them for being curious. She'd moved into their close-knit, old-fashioned midst, and they wanted to know what kind of person she was.

Lord, now they probably thought they did.

"I need a slate board," Zach said.

Cody tilted his head. "There's one in the attic."

Zach's head came up. He'd been muttering to himself, unaware of Cody's presence in the room. He'd stationed himself at a small table in Cody's bedroom. The tools he'd brought along with him lay scattered around him on the table. The device, too, was there. Its protective cover removed, and its insides exposed as he checked to be sure it hadn't been damaged coming through the portal. The leather-bound journal with his notes inside was open, and a newfangled ballpoint pen lay beside it. Zach had already filled three new pages with his account of his trip.

"Cody. Just the man I want to see."

"Really?"

"Yes, indeed. I'm having some trouble with your modern vernacular. Tell me, son, what does it mean when a woman refers to a man as a, uh, hunk?"

Cody grinned. "Means he's handsome."

Zach felt his brows lift in surprise. "Handsome?"

"Verrrry handsome," Cody said. "Did my mom call you a hunk, Zach?"

"Er…no. No, of course not. I read it in a book, actually."

"Uh-huh."

Zach actually felt his face heat. So Jane found him to be…handsome. Verrrry handsome. It wasn't such a major revelation. And it certainly shouldn't be this pleasing to have confirmation of what he'd already suspected. He cleared his throat. "You were telling me about the attic?" he prompted, in an effort to change the subject.

"Yeah," Cody was saying. "There's lots of neat stuff up there. A big safe, and some old furniture. But I don't know why you need a chalkboard."

"Ah, yes, my safe." Zach frowned. No doubt everything in it was worthless today. And it occurred to him that he was, for the second time in his life, lusting after a woman who was far wealthier than he. That thought troubled him more than it should. He cleared his throat. "The slate board. I need it for calculations, Cody. My work involves complicated mathematical problems, and it's easier to work them out if I have..." He let his voice trail off, because Cody had turned away from him and yanked open a drawer.

"How come you don't just use this?" He showed Zach a small unit, a bit smaller and thinner than Zach's device.

"What...?"

"It's a calculator," Cody told him. He turned so that Zach could view the tiny screen on the thing, and he pressed numbered buttons. "Watch this. One hundred fifty-three times forty-five divided by 56.9 plus two. Equals...." He pressed the button with the equal sign and held the box up to Zach.

It read 123.0017574. Zach shook his head slowly, and turned to the table, rapidly doing the figuring on a sheet of scrap paper. Amazingly, he came up with the same answer.

"It's gonna be a lot faster this way," Cody said, and he set the calculator down on the table beside Zach's journal. "I'm really sorry about Benjamin." Cody pulled up a chair, close beside Zach's, and sat down.

A huge lump rose in Zach's throat as he recalled, vividly, the way Ben used to work at his side before he became too weak from the illness to do so any longer. That was when Zach had moved his table and tools into his son's bedroom. So that they could work together the way they used to.

"I want to help," Cody said.

Zach blinked at his burning eyes, and ruffled the boy's hair with one hand. "You're a good man, Cody. But I'm not sure what you can do."

"More than you think." Cody spun the chair he sat in around and wheeled it across the hardwood floor, stopping at the desk on the other end. "You haven't seen my computer yet."

"Another modern wonder?"

Cody nodded and flicked a switch. "I have a modem. We can talk to scientists all over the world, download all kinds of information. And you can feed in all your numbers, and try making changes on the computer before you try it on the real machine. That way, you might be able to figure out if something's gonna work before you go ahead and do it."

Zach braced one hand on the desk, blinking rapidly. "This machine...can do all that?"

Cody grinned. "Yeah."

"Are all children in this century as smart as you are, Cody?"

"Nah. I'm s'posed to be gifted."

Zach nodded, and drew his own chair over beside Cody's. "Well, it's a good thing. I'm beginning to feel decidedly uneducated. It does look as though this equipment of yours can save me a lot of time. So...will you teach me, Cody?"

Cody nodded hard, and it seemed to Zach the boy's spine lengthened and straightened. Zach watched and listened as Cody explained the machine to him. Part of him was wishing he could take the modern wonder apart to see what was going on inside it, what made it work. But he couldn't risk breaking it. Already he knew this piece of equipment would cut his research time by leaps and bounds. If he'd had access to this in his own time...

Perhaps he could find a way to avoid the side effects before he returned to the past. Or even a way to speed up the recharging process. And get back to his son all the sooner.

Jane found them together in Cody's room, hunched over the computer, and she stood there a moment, watching as Zach slowly punched keys and Cody looked at him with adoration in his eyes.

"Time to wash up for lunch, Codester," she said, startling them both.

"Okay, Mom." Cody smiled up at Zach. "We'll save this, Zach, and work on it some more later." Cody executed the save command, jumped out of his chair and rushed past Jane on his way to the bathroom down the hall. Zach got up, as well.

"Wait a minute," Jane said. "We need to talk."

Zach's brows rose, and he sat back down. Jane came into the room, glancing down the hall first, to be sure Cody was out of earshot. Then she took the seat her son had formerly occupied.

"Cody...he's a special boy."

"I can see that."

"His IQ is far above what's considered normal," she explained. "And from what I've read about you, I imagine yours is, too."

He shrugged, saying nothing.

"Zach, don't get too close to him."

He looked confused.

"Look, I don't want to see him get hurt. We both know you have to go back to your own time, eventually. But he's getting attached to you, I can see that already."

"Ah... I see what you're getting at. But, Jane, I

need the boy's help. With the use of this machine, I can—''

"I don't care about the machine, Zach. What I care about is my son.''

"Me, too," he said softly. And she felt a rush of guilt for objecting so strongly. Even more for what else was on her mind. She sighed, and lowered her head. "I know how important this is to you. I do. It's just...he's never had a father, Zach. And lately, all he's talked about is wanting one."

"I understand that," he said.

"No, you don't. You can't possibly. He's—''

"I understand, Jane." He sighed, and placed a hand on her shoulder. "Benjamin and Cody have more in common than you know. My Ben...he's never known a mother's love, and since he's been ill, it's all he's talked about. Wanting a mother. I understand everything you're saying."

He did, she realized slowly. She swallowed hard, looking him in the eye. "I'm sorry...about your wife, I mean."

Zach lowered his head, but not before she saw the bitterness flash in his eyes. She frowned at him. But he shook his head, seemingly eager to change the subject. "This drug," he said. "The one that can cure my son. Do you have any idea where I can obtain it?"

She drew a breath, lifted her chin. "I've been wanting to talk to you about that. Zach..."

"We can't get the medicine without a doctor helping us, can we, Mom?" They both turned to see Cody in the doorway, drying his small hands on a towel. "Don't you need a prescription?"

Zach's eyes met hers, and they were worried. "Yes," she said. "It's a powerful antibiotic, and a controlled substance. You can't buy it unless a doctor orders it."

"Then we'll contact a doctor," Zach said. "We'll explain, and—"

"And he'll have us all tossed into a rubber room," Jane said. It wasn't a good solution, and maybe it wasn't even a solution at all. More like a delaying tactic. When Zach only frowned, she explained, "He'll think we're nuts."

"Then we'll find another way." Zach's eyes were intense.

"We can look it up on the computer," Cody said. "Find out how to make the medicine, and—"

Zach shook his head. "We'd have the same set of problems, though. We don't have the supplies or equipment we'd need to create the drug. And if we didn't get it exactly right, it might not work at all. I can't risk failure."

Cody stood still, gnawing his lip. "Mom? You know how you said it was only okay to tell a lie when you really, really had to?"

She looked at her son through narrowed eyes. "Yeah?"

"Well, is it the same with, uh…with stealing?"

"Cody! You know it's never, ever all right to steal. Not ever!"

"Why, son?" Zach asked, going to Cody and kneeling in front of him. "Do you know where we can find some of these pills?"

"Sure. Doc Mulligan keeps all kinds of 'em in the little white cabinet at his office. 'Member, Mom?

When I had the strep throat? He just opened up his cabinet and got out a bottle of penicillin. He has lots of antibiotics in there.''

Zach looked at Jane. Cody looked at Jane.

"No.'' She shook her head firmly. They were still looking at her. "No, we're not doing it. Isn't it bad enough we have the whole town thinking I'm having—'' She bit her lip. "We're not going to convince them I'm a master burglar and a drug addict, as well.''

"We could leave money to pay for the pills, Mom. So it wouldn't *really* be stealing.''

"Cody Nicholas Fortune, I do not want to hear one more word about this. Do you understand? Not one word. No one in this house is stealing *anything, anywhere, anytime*. Got it?''

Cody's chin fell to his chest. "Yeah.''

"Good. Now…lunch is ready. Come on downstairs, the both of you.''

She sailed out of the room, and they followed.

"Perhaps,'' she heard Zach saying, "I could convince this good doctor to give me some of the pills. If I were to see him, I mean.''

"He's smart,'' Cody replied. "He always knows if you're faking it.''

"Well, maybe if I spoke to him. Where did you say his office was, Cody?''

Jane turned and glared at Zach, but Cody was already giving him detailed directions to Doc Mulligan's office. She couldn't put it off any longer. She had to talk to Zach, tell him why he couldn't go through with this. And she had to do it soon. Tonight, after Cody went to sleep.

Five

Zach needed rest. Jane had made up a spare bedroom for him to sleep in. He hadn't taken advantage of it yet, though every muscle in his body was aching to do just that. He was fairly certain he was running a fever. He felt slow and a bit groggy at times. But then, at other times, he felt perfectly fine. The symptoms did not seem to be easing as quickly as he had expected they would. Hopefully the research he was doing while he waited for the device to recharge would give him the answers he needed to avoid this kind of illness hitting him on the return trip.

The device. It sat on Cody's desk beside his computer, and Zach picked it up, held it in his palm. Hard to imagine that something this small could mean the difference between life and death for his son. Already it was beginning to recharge. It might even be strong enough to open the doorway now, though if it wasn't at full power, there would be something different awaiting him on the other side. He might go back farther than he'd intended, which wouldn't be too terrible. Then again, he might not get back far enough. And that would be disastrous. No use risking it. He didn't have the drug yet, anyway. Two more days. The device would be at full power, and it would send him back to the precise moment whence he'd come. And he'd save Benjamin's life.

He was glad that the time travel hadn't seemed to affect his intelligence. He'd picked up Cody's computer lessons very quickly, and spent half the night "inputting data," as the boy called it. Transferring all his notes and calculations onto the computer. With the boy's help, he'd contacted a physicist in Detroit, and "downloaded" some "software" that enabled the computer to perform the tasks Zach needed it to. It was amazing. Utterly amazing.

He'd nearly finished filling this thing with all his notes. Cody had fallen asleep on his child-size bed. Zach felt bad for having the light on and clicking the keys while the child tried to sleep. It was time for a break, anyway. His eyes were beginning to glaze over.

He went to the bed, bent over it and gently slipped his arms beneath the sleeping child. When he picked him up, he was painfully reminded of Benjamin, so weak he could barely get out of bed anymore without Zach's help. Cody was heavy by comparison, and the age difference wasn't solely responsible for that, as Zach knew all too well.

He looked down at Cody's freckle-spattered face and red curls. And his heart squeezed tight. Lowering his head, he kissed the child's forehead. Zach wondered whether Cody's father were truly dead, or whether he'd simply abandoned his child the way Claudia had abandoned Benjamin. If he had, Zach thought grimly, he was a fool. To have a son like Cody and a woman like Jane... Any sane man would kill to keep them. Not walk away.

He stepped into the hallway, carried Cody to the guest room Jane had made up for him, then lowered him gently into that bed. He'd sleep more soundly here, without the light and the clicking keys. He tucked Cody in, and the boy stirred, opened his eyes and peered up at Zach.

"I wish," he said, his voice slurred with sleepiness, "I could have a dad like you."

Zach blinked the inexplicable burning that sprang into his eyes. "If I could, my boy, I'd make you my own." Cody smiled and fell back into a deep sleep. But Zach only stood there, shocked at the words that had just fallen from his lips. Make Cody his own? And Jane, as well? Good Lord, what kind of foolish fancy had come over him just now? For just an instant, though, the thought had occurred to him, and now he couldn't get it out of his mind. The thought that he could take them both back with him when he opened that doorway the day after tomorrow. Make his son well, and give him the mother he'd been wishing for. And an older brother to boot. That he could keep Jane Fortune, that incredible mixture of modern woman and old-fashioned girl, by his side, make her a part of his life, for always...

Ridiculous. Not only did he have no use for a woman in his life, he had no delusions that Jane would agree to such a scheme. To leave her modern conveniences, her microwave, her automobile? To take Cody from his computers and Nintendo games? Half of what the child had learned in his life wasn't even known in Zach's time. No, it was a foolish notion, and one best left unexplored. He had his son, and his work. And that was all he needed. All he'd ever needed.

He returned to Cody's computer screen, working some more, waiting, as he'd been waiting all night, for the sound of Jane's footsteps as she walked past on her way to bed. He glanced down at the note he'd made earlier, when he asked Cody if he knew the name of the drug that would cure quinaria. And, of course, the boy genius had readily supplied it. Tryptonine. He had everything he needed to proceed, but he couldn't do a damned thing until Jane was asleep. A glimpse at his watch told him it was after eleven, and she still hadn't retired. What was she waiting for?

The door opened, and Jane stood there, a cup of fragrant coffee in her hand. "I saw the light was still on," she said. "Thought you could use sustenance." When she came in, he saw the plate of cookies in her other hand. And his stomach growled a welcome.

"Thank you, Jane."

"Are you going to stay at this all night?"

"I want to be ready. When the device has recharged, I need to be ready to use it. If I can find an explanation for these side effects before then, all the better."

She nodded. "I know that, but Zach, you won't do Benjamin any good at all if you work yourself until you collapse." She lifted the cup, and he took it, his hand touching hers. Jane frowned, quickly looking down at his hand. Then she came closer, pressed a palm to his forehead, and then to his cheek.

He liked her this close to him. He liked her touching him.

"You're burning up!"

"You're exaggerating. It's only a slight fever."

Her brows rose, twin arches over beautiful eyes that he could have spent a very long time looking into. "So what is it? Are you coming down with quinaria fever, too?"

"No. I had it as a child and somehow survived, so I'm immune. This is just...another side effect, I suppose."

She set the plate of cookies on the table and left the room, returning seconds later with a pair of small white tablets, which she gave to him. "Take these. They'll help with the fever."

He did. And then he snatched up a cookie and dunked it.

"Zach, have you thought about what's going to happen to you when you go back through that...that portal of yours? If you don't find a way to avoid the side effects, I mean?"

He averted his eyes. "No way of telling. I've been trying to understand exactly what it was about the portal that caused these reactions, but so far, I just don't know."

"You don't look any better than you did when you arrived. Worse, in fact."

He shook his head. "No, it's no worse. Not much better, but a little. Perhaps I'll build up a tolerance, so that when I go back the side effects will be less pronounced."

"Or maybe it will get worse every time, and you'll arrive back there barely able to function."

"That's not a consideration, Jane. As long as I get

the drug back to Benjamin, I really don't care what ill effects I suffer.''

"I know." She closed her eyes very briefly. Bit her lip, as if there were something there, about to jump out. A second later, her eyes opened again, and she drew a shaky breath. "But there are some other side effects—repercussions to what you're planning to do—that you haven't considered, Zach. And I think it's time you did."

Zach frowned down at her. "Something's bothering you about all of this. I knew that this morning. But, Jane, my son is dying. What else could possibly matter?"

Jane lowered her head, and Zach caught her chin, lifted it, searched her beautiful eyes. "You don't want me to go back. Why, Jane?"

She parted her lips, but closed them again.

"It's all right. I think I know why." And then, very slowly, he lowered his head, and touched her lips with his. They trembled against his mouth, and the desire he'd felt for her all along came flooding back, swamping him, shaking him to the core. He slipped his arms around her slender waist and pulled her close to him, tight to his body. His mouth fed on hers as her lips parted. A tremulous sigh escaped her, and he inhaled it, relished it, as her arms crept around him. Her hands clasped his shoulders, and she arched against him.

Dazed and aroused beyond reason, Zach lifted his head. "I want you, Jane. I want you to the point of distraction."

He lifted one hand to thread his fingers in her hair,

while the other remained at the small of her back, holding her tight to him.

"I..." she breathed, and then stiffened, her eyes widening as she stared up at him. "No," she said softly, and there was no mistaking what he saw in those eyes. It was fear. "No, I won't fall...not again."

And then she turned and ran from the bedroom. Something compelled Zach to move. He lunged for the door and watched her run down the hall to her own room. Watched her go through the door, closing it hard behind her. And then he heard the gentle sounds of her bedsprings creaking as she lay down. He closed his eyes and told his imagination to behave itself. And while he was at it, he told his heart to go back to sleep, where it had been for the past six years, and to stop yearning for things it could never have.

God, he must be suffering mental, as well as physical, exhaustion for these thoughts to keep creeping in. He needed to sleep.

But not just yet. He had a mission tonight, and nothing, not even Jane and the fearful yearning in her eyes, was going to stop him from accomplishing it.

He was not the man she'd been wishing for. Not the father she'd longed for Cody to have and not the man of her dreams. He was a womanizer, dubbed the Don Juan of his time in one of the books she'd read. And even if that was an exaggeration, one fact could not be overlooked. He was going to leave her. Just as Greg had. She would not give in to the feelings that kept creeping in, like slow-moving waves eroding a sandy shore. She would not let her heart be broken again.

She wouldn't.

And yet she lay awake for hours, wishing that there was some way...

God, she hadn't even told him why he couldn't go ahead with his plan. And even when he realized how impossible it was, he'd still want to go back to his son, to be with him at the end. The thought brought tears to Jane's eyes. He'd hate her for what she had to tell him. Hate her for being the one to make him realize that it was his son's destiny to die, and thereby save countless lives. Hate her. He'd hate her.

And it was going to kill her to see that emotion in his eyes when she told him.

She couldn't sleep. She felt sick to her stomach, and after tossing and turning restlessly she got up, intending to go downstairs, maybe do some pacing, and rehearse the words she would use to deliver the blow that might very well destroy Zachariah Bolton.

She tiptoed down the hall, but when she came to the door of the bedroom where Zach was sleeping, she found her feet wouldn't go any farther. It was stupid. He was asleep by now. No light came from beneath the closed door. But she couldn't go past without at least peeking in, just glancing at him as he lay there, drinking in the sight of him and wishing things could be different.

How had the man managed to get under her skin so thoroughly in so short a time?

She closed her hand around the doorknob, opened it gently. But the bed was empty. She stepped into

the room, snapping on the light, but Zach wasn't
there. And a gnawing sensation in the pit of her
stomach told her he wasn't anywhere else in the
house, either. She had a damned good idea of where
he had gone. After she'd expressly told him not to.
To Dr. Mulligan's office, a few miles away. Probably
on foot.

Jane closed her eyes and pressed her fingertips to
her forehead. Damn him. He had no business being
out alone, trying to break and enter, in the condition
he was in. No business at all. He could collapse in
the street, and then what would happen? Suppose he
woke up with no memory again and started rambling
on about 1897 and Aunt Hattie's credenza? They'd
toss him into a mental ward, for God's sake.

She searched the ground floor, all the same, even
though she knew full well she wouldn't find him
there. Then she paced the living room. She should
go after him. She really should. He could be hurt or
sick or delirious somewhere. Or in jail. Oh, for
heaven's sake, and what was she supposed to say
when she found him? How was she going to explain
that she'd known he'd gone out? Was she going to
confess that she'd been lonely and restless and unable to sleep? Was she going to admit that she'd
slipped out of bed and tiptoed down the hallway in
the dead of night, and that she'd quietly eased the
bedroom door open so that she could look at him as
he slept?

No way in hell.

But she couldn't very well leave Cody alone to go
after him, either. And she couldn't wake her son up,

or the little mischief-maker would want to go along on Zach's crime spree. He'd want to...

An odd little feeling rippled up her spine and into the back of her neck. A feeling only another mother would understand. Frowning, she tilted her head, narrowed her eyes. Cody...

She hurried up to the guest room where Cody had been sleeping and slipped inside, and then she had what felt distinctly like heart palpitations.

Cody's bed was empty.

"Zach, look out!"

Zach dropped to his knees automatically at the harsh whisper. And then he turned, squinting through the darkness at the small body that had landed there beside him. An automobile passed, its headlamps brushing the bushes in front of them with white light, then fading in the distance.

Zach gripped Cody's shoulders, staring into his freckled face in stark disbelief. "What in the name of heaven are you doing here?"

"I followed you, Zach. Thought I could help. Did you get it?"

Zach pushed a hand through his hair. "If your mother finds out—"

"Did you get it?" Cody asked again, urgency in his tone.

"Yes. I got it."

"How?" Cody shook Zach's arm. "How, Zach?"

"I broke a window, reached through and unlocked the door. The cabinet was right where you told m—"

"You shoulda waited for me!" Cody rasped. "Darn it all, Zach, there's an alarm on that door. Doc has to punch in a code, even though he has a key. If you don't…I think the sheriff…''

"Let's get out of here." Taking Cody's arm, Zach raced around the building, through the damp grass. He crossed the road, in the darkness. His breaths made little puffs of steam.

"We'll never make it, Zach. That alarm probably went off as soon as you opened the darn door. Man, we shoulda brought my bike."

"Oh, sweet Jesus," Zach said, glancing at a vehicle in the distance with flashing red lights on the top. "Is that—?"

"Yeah, that's Sheriff O'Donnell. Boy, are we in trouble! My mom's gonna *kill* us." Cody turned in a circle, then paused, at the sight of another vehicle approaching rapidly from the opposite direction. "Look, Zach! I think it's… Yeah! It's Mom! C'mon!"

Gripping Zach's hand, Cody raced toward the approaching vehicle, and away from the one with the red lights. It was dark, and the sheriff's headlamps hadn't yet fallen on them. Zach didn't think the sheriff had seen them. Yet.

"She'll be mad as all get-out," Cody panted, still running and clinging to Zach's hand. "But at least she'll keep us outta jail!"

She couldn't believe it. She could not believe what she was seeing. Her son. Her ten-year-old genius son, running away from a police car in the middle of the night, like some kind of fugitive. She gunned the accelerator, sped up beside them and skidded to a stop.

Cody yanked the back door open, and the two of them dived into the back seat just as Quigly O'Donnell's cruiser pulled up beside Jane's car.

"Sit there and look innocent," she ordered. She rolled her window down as Quigly sauntered across the street, looking serious.

"Hello, Sheriff," she said, and tried to sound cheerful, which was difficult, given the fact that she was grating her teeth behind her smile.

"Well, now, Jane Fortune! What in the world are you doing driving around town this time of the night?" He braced his hands on the driver's door and leaned closer.

"Couldn't sleep," she blurted.

Quigly frowned. "Ayuh. And they couldn't, either?" He nodded to the two in the back seat.

"Oh...well, no. None of us could. You see, my, uh...my cat disappeared today, and we were worried. So we decided to drive around and see if we could find her." It was, she thought, the perfect answer. Quigly O'Donnell was a known animal lover. She caught Cody's smirk in the rearview mirror and realized he'd caught her lying again. Fine example of motherhood she was turning out to be.

"That's too bad," the sheriff said, rubbing his chin with one hand. "And here I didn't even know you *had* a cat. Any sign of her?"

"No, not yet."

"Well, now, don't you worry. Just give me a description, and I'll keep an eye out."

"Uh...sure. She's, um..."

"Black," Cody helpfully supplied. Unfortunately,

he blurted it out at the same moment his mother said, "White" and Zach said, "Cinnamon."

Jane shot the two bigmouths a glare, then turned to the sheriff again, smiling. "Calico."

"I see. She wearin' a collar?"

"Shouldn't this wait for another time, Sheriff? I don't want to keep you. You were obviously on business." She nodded toward the still-flashing lights.

"Ayuh, but nothing too urgent. Doc Mulligan's alarm went off again. Third time this month. I have to head over there and check it out, but I do believe he has a critter living in his office. Sets off the motion detector when it crosses the beam, you know. Squirrel or a mouse or something. Say, why did you pull over out here? Did you see something?"

"Uh...no. I mean...just your lights. I thought it was the law, you know, pulling over when..."

"Well, not when you're headin' the opposite direction."

"Oh."

He stuck his head right in her window. "You must be Bolton. I heard you were, er...staying with *Miss* Fortune."

"Renting a room, actually. Good to meet you, Sheriff." Zach thrust one hand over the seat to shake Quigly's.

"Renting a room, eh?" It was obvious the man doubted that little ploy. "Well, it's a pleasure, Bolton. I'd best be on my way, take a look around the doc's place." He touched the brim of his hat. "I'll keep an eye out for that cat of yours, Jane."

"Night," she said, and pulled the car into gear.

* * *

She paced. Back and forth across the sizable living room, crossing between Zach's easy chair and the red-orange glow in the fireplace, again and again. And he watched, waited, feeling a bit the way he had when Headmistress Landon had caught him smuggling that pet mouse into primary school so long ago. Although Miss Landon had never looked quite as attractive as Jane did right now. She was even prettier in her anger, and that struck him as unusual in a woman. Her eyes sparkled with it. Her smooth cheeks had taken on a cherry gleam, and her lips were slightly parted.

Cody had wisely chosen to obey without question when she sent him straight up to bed. The little hellion got him in all sorts of hot water and then skinned out at the first opportunity, leaving Zach to face the music alone.

Smart boy.

Oh, well. At least it had given him the chance to see Jane this way. It wasn't a sight he'd forget anytime soon.

She paused in her pacing and looked at him. He decided to face the music, cleared his throat and said, "I had no idea Cody was following me."

She rolled her eyes, shook her head.

"I slipped out very quietly, Jane. I thought you were both sound asleep. I wouldn't involve the boy in a theft. You must believe that."

Her eyes narrowed.

"I have a son of my own, Jane. I'm a parent, too."

That soft chin came down, the clenched jaw eased a little, and air rushed from her lips in a sigh. "I know. Okay, Zach, I believe you. But I told you not to—''

''Try to imagine yourself in my place, just for a moment.''

Jane's thickly lashed eyes slammed closed, as if, perhaps, she didn't want to imagine any such thing. But, perhaps, was doing so anyway.

''Your son—your Cody—lies dying of the fever. And a mile from you, under lock and key, is a drug that can save him. Would you go after it?'' He got to his feet and went to her, cradled her chin in his palm and lifted it, very gently, so that he could look into those stunning eyes. ''Would you, Jane, even though some very beautiful, very wise person had advised against it?''

She held his gaze. ''You know I would.''

He smiled, nodding as his hand fell to his side again. ''And I knew you'd answer honestly. I have it now, Jane.'' He took the small plastic pill bottle from his pocket, set it on the coffee table and stared at it, barely able to contain his joy. ''I can save my Benjamin. If I can just get back to him, I can—''

''No, Zach,'' she whispered. ''No, you can't.''

He frowned and felt his smile slowly die. ''Of course I can.''

''Zach…'' She shook her head as if in frustration. ''Look, there's something I haven't told you. I thought it could wait until you were feeling better, stronger— No, that's a lie. I was waiting because I didn't want to tell you. I couldn't find the words, and I don't want to see the hatred in your eyes when I—'' She bit her lip.

''Jane.'' She stopped her rambling, looked at him,

and to Zach's surprise there were tears standing in her eyes. His own reflection shimmered in them. The sight of those tears alarmed him beyond all common sense. So much so that he found himself gripping her shoulders, searching her face. "My God, Jane, what is it?"

She sniffed once, and then seemed to draw herself up. "Quinaria fever was cured because of Benjamin's death," she told him. "When you disappeared, Zach, your colleagues, Waterson and Bausch, came together. Instead of competing against one another, they worked together to develop a cure, and they did. They did it in tribute to you, Zach, and to your loss. The loss of all those other lives was never enough to inspire them the way the loss of a man they considered to be the finest scientific mind of their time did. They thought you'd gone insane when Benjamin died, and you disappeared. They blamed it on the fever."

Zach blinked down at her, shaking his head in disbelief.

"It's all here," she said as she turned from him to pick up the large book that laid on the table. "Zach, if you save your son, those men won't find a cure. Maybe no one will. If you change the past that way—" she shook her head slowly "—then what becomes of the present? How many hundreds of people will die? And how many thousands of their descendants will never be born? What about—"

"Stop!" Zach turned away from her, pressing his hands to his ears. Because he couldn't bear to hear her, and know she was right. So right, and yet she hadn't even touched on the magnitude of the implications. The way the life—or the death—of one little boy could change the world as she knew it. The succession of other research that had likely sprung from what science learned in curing one disease had probably led to cures for several others. All of that might be lost. And the victims those diseases took....some of them might turn out to be today's most influential figures. What would Jane's world look like if they'd never been born, because their ancestors had died of something that should have been cured?

Soft hands came to his shoulders from behind. They squeezed, and then Jane's head lowered to rest lightly against his back. "I'm sorry."

"I can't..." he said, then had to pause to clear his throat. "I can't simply give up, Jane. There has to be a way."

"You can't change history without impacting the present...and the future. Anything you do in the past is going to have repercussions, Zach. It's like throwing a pebble into still water. The ripples go on and on."

He turned around, facing her. "I will not allow my child to die when I have the means to save him."

"I know it's—"

"I can't, Jane. And I *won't*."

"You're a scientist. Think about what could happen, Zach, think about mankind."

"I don't give a damn about mankind!" he shouted. "I want my son!" And then his knees seemed to buckle beneath him, and he found himself on the floor, one fisted hand on the easy chair to keep himself upright. He closed his eyes and let his chin fall, because he couldn't bear for this strong woman to see him cry. "I just want my son," he whispered once more.

Before he saw her move, she was kneeling there with him, facing him. Her arms slipped around his waist, silk-wrapped steel. She drew him closer, like a mother cradling her child, and she held him to her breast, rocking slowly as her palms made soothing patterns over his back and shoulders. "I know," she whispered. "I know, Zach, I know."

His cheeks were damp, but he wasn't certain whether the tears were hers or his own. "I can't give up on him, Jane. Sweet Jesus forgive me, but I can't." He twisted his arms around her, clinging to her as if to salvation.

"Maybe there *is* a way." She turned her face to his, kissed his mouth, drank their mingled tears from his lips. She lifted her head, searching his eyes. "I've been going crazy trying to think of some way...and if there is, Zach, we'll find it. I promise you that. But if there isn't..."

"There has to be!" He held her tighter.

Her sob was wrenched from her breast, and she buried her face in his neck. They knelt like that for a long moment, clinging to each other as Jane cried softly. Finally she sniffed, and straightened. "For now, Zach, just for now, rest. You're sick and exhausted and half out of your mind. Rest."

Zach lifted his head to stare into Jane's eyes. He couldn't hate her, couldn't even be angry with her for what she'd pointed out. It was nothing less than the truth. Her tear-dampened eyes met his, clung to them as if in a spiritual embrace. She got to her feet then and, bending low, she took his hands and drew him up, as well. Taking three steps backward, Jane stopped when she stood beside the sofa, still not letting go. So Zach let his numb legs carry him where she led. He sat down when she guided his body to do so. He felt dazed, shocked. His mind swirled as he sought a solution, but he was too devastated to see one.

She knelt in front of him and took off his shoes, peeled the socks away. ''Put your feet up, Zachariah. Go on.''

He did as she said. His mind buzzed. What if he— No, that wouldn't work. Jane seemed to melt away, only to return a second later with pills in her palm. She tucked them between his lips. Her fingers tasted salty and cool. He took the drink she offered, swallowed the tablets, his mind still awash in possibilities. Seemed Jane Fortune had a pill for everything. But not one to cure this nightmare. Maybe nothing could.

Jane sat on the end of the sofa, and she caught his shoulders, drawing him downward until his head rested in her lap. And he thought very briefly of the silken thighs beneath his cheek, and the way he'd like to touch them...kiss them. Anything to forget this awful pain.

She pressed her forefingers to his temples and began rubbing tiny circles there. Sleep came slowly, as he stared up at her looking down at him. Her face became the face of an angel, and then blurred and dissolved into nothingness.

Cody sat at the top of the stairs, and he tried not to cry like a baby, the way the grown-ups had. All his life, all he'd wanted was a little brother. Someone he could watch out for, and play with, and teach. And since Zach had come here, he'd begun to feel like he really had one. Little Benjamin, just a few years younger, sick and needing help. Sure, he was far away, out of reach, but Cody still felt close to him. He'd felt like a big brother as he helped Zach find a way to save little Ben. And then those stupid grown-ups had to go and ruin it with all their "good of mankind" talk.

A kid was dying, for crying out loud! There would be enough time to think about the good of mankind later. Right now...that little guy back in 1897 needed someone. And right now, it seemed like Cody was the only someone Benjamin had.

No. He wasn't going to just sit around and let the grown-ups decide what was best. They didn't understand. They just...they just didn't get it.

Cody slipped down the stairs, quiet as a mouse. He sneaked to the coffee table, and he reached out, keeping his eyes on his mom just about the whole time. Zach wouldn't wake. He was out cold, and snoring like a chain saw. Mom might, though. She was a light sleeper most of the time. But she'd dozed off, too, and she didn't stir as he crept forward. Cody's hand closed around the brown plastic bottle. He drew his arm to his side, and sneaked away, up the stairs, and finally into his room. He only sighed in relief when the door was closed behind him.

Phew. That was the hard part. The rest, he decided, would be easy as pie. He went to the table, and picked up Zach's remote-control box. Pretty simple. Two knobs.

He turned one of them.

Six

Something woke Jane up. It might have been the fact that Zachariah Bolton now lay facedown in her lap. Her dorm shirt had somehow bunched up around her hips, and his face rested against her naked thighs and silk panties. She felt every whisker as his soft snores blew warm breath in places that hadn't been breathed on in ages. Places that came to life and let Jane know they resented the neglect they'd suffered of late. She automatically shifted, trying to extricate herself from the awkward position, but her movements only made matters worse. Zach stirred. The change in his breathing patterns told her he was awake. But he took his time about sitting up. And when he finally did, she almost wished he hadn't, because the look in his dark eyes when they met hers made her stomach twist.

She half expected a smart remark. But he didn't smirk as he stared up at her. The sun was just beginning to rise, and the deep orange blush painted his face and glinted in his eyes.

"I've never been so afraid in my life," he told her.

"Neither have I." She lifted one hand to brush his sable hair away from his forehead.

"You?" His brows went up. "Why, Jane?"

She swallowed hard, deciding she had to tell him the rest. All of it. "I didn't tell you everything last night, Zach."

He closed his eyes. "Then don't do it now. Damnation, Jane, I don't think I could stand much more."

"You have to."

He sat up slowly, facing her. "Coffee first," he said, and as he did, he ran the backs of his fingers down one side of her face, stroking it as if he were deriving some sort of pleasure from doing so. "At least let me wake up thoroughly before you give me any more to worry about. I'm still a little dazzled by the dream I was having." His gaze dipped to caress her thighs once more, and she hastily got to her feet, yanking the dorm shirt down where it belonged. "Besides, I'm still not over the shock of how much undergarments have changed in the past century," he went on slowly. "I like those you're wearing. Silk, are they? They felt like it against my face."

She'd have shot him down with a cutting reply, if not for the pain she could still see in his eyes. He was only avoiding the subject at hand. She knew that. He was afraid to discuss it just yet, afraid of the time when he'd be forced to admit that he couldn't take the drug back to save his son. And so he was putting it off. Delaying what he must realize was inevitable.

"I'll make that coffee," she said, turning for the kitchen.

"I'm acting like an ass," he muttered, and he followed her. "And it's doing me no good. You're obviously not a woman who melts at pretty words."

"I'm not a woman interested in petty affairs, either."

He tilted his head, narrowed his eyes. "And yet you're lonely, aren't you, Jane? I'm sure I've never met a woman as lonely as you."

She averted her eyes, because his words were like blades that drove through to the bone. "Don't be ridiculous. I have Cody."

"And I have Benjamin. A boy I love more than...than life itself. But that doesn't mean I'm not lonely."

She blinked, and swung her gaze up to meet his. "You?"

"You're right about petty affairs, Jane Fortune. They only leave you more empty than before."

Shaking her head in confusion, Jane turned away from him. She yanked the carafe from the coffee maker and held it under the faucet, filling it with water. But when she turned, he was there, lounging against the counter, watching her with something speculative and curious in his eyes.

"Why don't you tell me about Cody's father?"

"Why do you want to know?" She continued what she was doing, pouring the water into the coffee maker, then removing the basket and reaching for the filters.

"It was unusual, in my time at least, for a woman to bear a child out of wedlock, raise him on her own, and still manage to hold the respect of her neighbors. Yet the people here seem to hold you in high regard."

"Yeah, well, they did until you showed up." She couldn't get a single filter separated from the rest of the stack, though she kept trying. "More has changed in the past century than underwear, Zach."

He smiled at her, but it was a sad smile. They both knew what they were doing. Making small talk. Avoiding the issue. With his tousled hair and rumpled clothes, he looked like a little boy. Well, maybe not quite. Still, he seemed vulnerable—enough so that she was having trouble working up to telling him the rest of it.

He came a step closer, and reached past her to take the stack of coffee filters from her hands. Deftly he peeled one from the pile, handed it to her, then returned the rest to their spot in the cupboard. "Tell me," he said, "about Cody's father."

Sighing, Jane wondered why it was so difficult to break free of his gaze when he looked at her that way. So intently. As if she were the very center of the universe. No wonder the women of his time had fallen at his feet. She tucked the filter into the basket, opened the coffee canister and fished out the scoop. "I was young, and gullible. He was a smooth-talking lady-killer in sheep's clothing. A lot like you, actually."

"Like me?" His brows went up.

Jane had to focus hard to keep track of how many scoops of coffee she'd dumped into the basket. She slid it into the coffee maker and switched the machine on.

"Were you in love with him, Jane?"

She shrugged. "I thought so at the time. He said he loved me, but it was just a line."

"A line," he repeated.

"Just a phrase he used to get me into bed." She turned to face him, leaning back against the counter. His eyes widened a little—probably, she figured, at what she'd said. No doubt the ladies of his time hadn't used such straightforward terms about sex. "He pretended to be an idealist. He was a musician, with a band, and they wrote songs about the troubles of our times, moral bankruptcy, war, that kind of thing. And I fell for it, hook, line and sinker." She shrugged her shoulders. "I told him I was pregnant about the same time he and his band were offered a lot of money to sign with a record producer. He said he couldn't put his career on hold, not when it was just taking off. He hopped a plane, leaving me and all those sterling ideas of his in the dust."

Zach tilted his head. "He left you, alone and carrying his son?" Jane nodded, and Zach's jaw twitched. "He was not only an irresponsible dog, Jane, but a fool."

She drew a breath and sighed. "You're right, he was a fool. Cody is a miracle. Greg never realized he was turning up his nose at the greatest gift he'd ever receive."

"You speak of him in the past tense."

She licked her lips. "His band was a one-hit wonder. They recorded an album that didn't sell, went on a tour that ended up being canceled. The band flopped, and he couldn't take it. Died of a drug overdose within a few months."

Zach's lips thinned. "He wasn't worthy of a son like Cody," he said, and he reached out, closing his hand around hers, squeezing gently. "Or of a woman like you, Jane."

"At least he taught me a valuable lesson," she said, drawing her hand away, though reluctantly.

"Never to trust a man again?"

The coffee gurgled into the pot and spread its aroma throughout the kitchen. Jane shook her head. ''I know better than to let myself care for a man who's going to walk out on me in the end,'' she told him. And then, lowering her head, she added, ''Or...I thought I did.''

He leaned forward, bracing his hands on the countertop on either side of her. His lips brushed over the top of her head, and then his arms came around her to hold her, very gently. ''I thought I'd learned a lot of things, too, Jane. But you're testing every one of them.''

Blinking in surprise, she looked up quickly. His face was very close to hers, and his body only a hairsbreadth away. Every cell in her urged her to press closer, just a little. Just enough so she could really feel him there. She clenched her jaw and closed her eyes. ''I can't do this, Zach,'' she whispered. ''It'll kill me when you go.'' And then she blinked, and desire was replaced by heartache for what she had to tell him. What she knew it would do to him. ''If you go,'' she went on. ''Once I explain...''

She felt him move away from her before she opened her eyes. He stood two feet from her now, staring at her, shaking his head. ''*If?* I *have* to go. Dammit, Jane, I'm trying to save my son's life.''

''And I'm trying to save mine.''

He frowned at her. ''I don't understand.''

''I've been thinking about this all night, Zach. And even if you do go back, even if you give that drug to your son, I can't see how it will work. If Benjamin is saved, your colleagues won't be moved to work together to find a cure for the fever. Maybe no one else will be successful. Maybe there will be no cure, and if there isn't, then it couldn't have been in Doc's office for you to steal. It couldn't have been here for you to take back to Benjamin. You'll lose him anyway. Don't you see? Everything you do will cancel out everything you've done. It can't work.''

Zach turned in a slow circle, shaking his head. ''No. No, you have it wrong. Those men were meant to develop the drug, and they will still do it.''

''But what if they don't?''

''Then someone else will.''

''Maybe. But maybe not. And then—''

''It won't matter. Once I give the drug to Benjamin, he'll be well. It won't reverse itself—I'm sure of it, Jane. I can save him.''

Jane licked her lips, drew in a steadying breath. ''And what about what I said to you last night, Zach? What about all the people who have been sick with the fever since then? What becomes of them, if the cure isn't developed?''

''The hell with them!'' he shouted, pushing both hands back through his hair. The look of torment on his face was almost more than she could bear.

Jane moved forward, and put her hand on his shoulder. She didn't want to do this. Wished she could avoid it with everything in her. But she couldn't. ''You don't mean that.''

''I do. I can't—''

''Zach, when Cody was two years old, I nearly lost him. He was so sick I didn't think he'd pull through. And it—''

"No..." He took a step away from her, staring down in horror. "Don't, Jane...."

She bit her lip to stop its trembling, but there was nothing she could do to prevent the tears that filled her eyes. "Yes. It was quinaria. And if it hadn't been for that drug, Cody would have died." She lowered her head, biting back a sob that managed to escape anyway, and suddenly his arms came around her, drawing her closer, holding her to his chest, and she felt him shaking. "I know it's selfish, Zach, but I'm so afraid. If you go back, if you save your son, I might just lose mine."

Zach cradled her against him, held her tight, as if trying to shield her, and himself, from this horrible dilemma. The nightmare was beyond them, outside the circle of his arms, and as long as he didn't let her go, it couldn't get in. She cried softly, her tears wetting her cheeks, so that when she tipped her head up, when he kissed her, he tasted their salt, as well as her sweetness. He drank the misery from her mouth, and she fed on his in exchange. They clung, tears mingling, two strangers sharing one nightmare. And he couldn't stop kissing her. Wouldn't stop. Because when he did, when this tiny interlude that was serving as a refuge ended, he'd have to face reality again. And he couldn't. He couldn't.

His mouth never leaving hers, he moved backward until he reached the swinging doors that separated kitchen from living room. One hand groped, found a wooden spoon, and deftly slid it into place, linking the two door handles together so that no one could walk in. And then he returned his hands to her hair, burying his fingers deeply, twisting them in the satin of it. He bent over her, arching her backward, sliding his tongue between her lips to taste her.

He felt her heart pounding, felt the way she arched against him. And sensed her desperation, knew it, because it was his own, as well. She clung to him as if to life, to sanity, to hope. And when his mouth moved down over her throat, her hands slid into his hair, to draw him even closer.

He slipped his hands down her body, tracing the swells of her breasts, the curve of her waist. He moved over her hips to her thighs, until he met bare skin, and then he gathered the nightshirt she wore and lifted it. Kept lifting it as his caress skimmed upward again, his palms tingling over her warm flesh, and finally tugging the garment over her head. He dropped it to the floor and stared down at her, naked now, aside from the silk underwear. At her breasts, bare and beautiful and perfect. He touched them, closed his hands over them, and then closed his eyes and moaned deep in his throat. This desperation had become desire, so potent and strong he thought it would kill him if he didn't sate it soon. He grasped her legs, lifted them up and around him, and moved forward until her buttocks slid over the countertop. His hands pushing her panties down before he stepped between her parted thighs. She arched backward, offering what he craved, and he dipped his head, taking the very tip of one luscious breast into his mouth, nursing at it with ever-growing hunger, devouring and pulling at her nipple until she panted and cried. He was so hard, so in need of her it was painful, and while he worried her other breast, he slipped one hand between her legs, parting and testing the slick heat there. And then teasing the core of her desire until her hands came to his trousers, frantically working the buttons free, shoving them downward. She gripped his buttocks with both hands and pulled him forward, plunging him into her so fast and so deep that he groaned aloud.

He found her mouth again, took it, savored it as he moved with her. The pace of his thrusts gained speed, and force, but still he wanted more of her. More of her. He'd never have enough. He gripped her hips and lifted her off the counter, pulling her down farther, her own weight driving him deeper inside her. And she linked her arms and her legs around him, and began to move up and down, her hands tugging at his hair as her mouth became the voracious one that fed from his.

His knees buckled as every other part of him seemed to twist into tight little knots of pleasure so intense it was almost pain. And when he exploded inside her, he felt her climax adding to his, enhancing it. The rippling convulsions of her, milking him, drawing what felt like the very soul from his body along with his seed. And capturing it in her own.

He mouthed words he'd never uttered to a woman in his life. But not a sound emerged. They clung, and shuddered, and trembled with the aftershocks of that incredible lovemaking for a long time.

And then she lifted her head, and she kissed his mouth, and she gently lowered herself until she was standing on her feet again. And…and she was crying.

He wanted to take away her pain, and didn't know how. But all he could say was ''There has to be a way. We'll find a way. We can save them both, Jane. We must.''

She stared deeply into his eyes, her tears brimming and burning holes through his heart. ''You're going through with this? Even though it might cost my son his life?''

''*Might* cost his life, Jane.'' He stroked her hair, kissed her again. And again. Held her naked, trembling body in his arms and wished with everything in him that he'd never have to let go. ''But I have no doubt that my son *will* lose his life if I don't. I have to try.''

Trailing her hand down his damp cheek, she whispered, ''I'm sorry, Zach. But I won't let you. I can't let you do this.''

And they stood there, aching for each other, and for themselves. Each willing to do whatever it took to protect their child. They just stared, and he knew this was destroying her as surely as it was destroying him. He couldn't even be angry with her for what she'd said, what she'd no doubt try to do.

Shaking his head with regret, he reached past her, picked up her nightshirt and, with exquisite tenderness, put it over her head. She tucked her arms into one sleeve, then the other, as he held them for her. And he lowered the garment until its hem brushed her thighs, as before.

A loud knock at the door made her whirl. Zach saw the sheriff from the night before, Quigly O'Donnell, standing there with a ball of fur cradled in his arms.

Jane's eyes shot to Zach's, wide, and he knew she

was wondering how long the sheriff had been standing there, peering through the glass into the kitchen.

Zach shook his head. "I would have seen him, Jane. He wasn't there."

With a sigh of relief, she moved forward and opened the door.

"Found your cat," the sheriff said, thrusting the multicolored beast into her arms. "Don't think she likes riding much. Clawed my upholstery up like you wouldn't believe."

Jane blinked down at the animal, but said only, "Thank you."

God, her voice sounded dead.

"Mornin', Bolton," Quigly offered.

"Good morning."

"Say, Jane, what in the name of all hell is that boy of yours up to?"

Jane frowned, and Zach came to stand very close beside her, alert. "Cody's still sleeping," Jane said. "Why?"

Quigly chuckled and shook his head. "Ayuh. Now, maybe. But I'm thinking you ought to sneak on upstairs and look in on him all the same, Jane. Judgin' by the flash of light I saw coming from his bedroom window when I drove past here a few hours ago, I'd say he short-circuited his computer or something."

"Flash of..." Jane's eyes widened, and she looked at Zach. He knew the panic that was surging in her, because he was feeling it, too.

"Keep tabs on that cat now, you hear?" Sheriff O'Donnell turned from the door and sauntered back to his cruiser.

Jane's knees started to buckle. Zach saw the way she sagged, and he gripped her shoulders, steadied her. She was shaking like a leaf, and whiter than chalk, but she stiffened and started through the kitchen, the cat still cradled in her arms. Her steps quickened as she moved, and Zach kept pace. By the time she reached the foot of the stairs, she was running.

"Cody!" she called. "Cody, answer me!"

She burst through the doorway at the top of the stairs. But the room was empty. Jane swung her head this way and that, scanning the entire room, whispering Cody's name once more in what came out as a hopeless gasp. And then she went still. Zach followed her gaze to the device, lying in the very center of the floor. Its back cover had popped off, and wires sprung from inside.

Slowly Zach moved past her to stand at the spot in the center of the room. He felt the static electricity teasing the hairs at his nape, sensed the remaining charge in the air here. A low yowl came from the frightened cat, and it leaped from Jane's arms and ran from the room.

"The doorway's been opened," he said slowly. "Within the last few hours."

"No."

He bent to pick up the device, examined it, and swore under his breath.

"Is it..."

"Broken all to hell." He met her stricken eyes. "Looks as if Cody dropped it before he went through."

"Went...through?"

He held her gaze steadily, seeing the horror, the panic, the sickening feeling of helplessness, that he knew only too well. She shook her head in denial, tore her gaze from his and ran from the room. He heard her steps, her agonized cries, as she went from room to room, searching for her son. "Cody!" she shouted. "Cody, where are you? Answer me! Cody!"

Zach lowered his head in anguish. Two children, now, instead of one. And both of them might well be beyond his reach. Almighty God, the device hadn't even been up to full power when Cody used it. He might not have gone back to the moment Zach had left, but to sometime even earlier. He wasn't even certain he'd be able to find the child. Harsh breaths from the doorway drew his gaze upward, and he saw Jane there, her face already streaked with tears. He lifted a hand, took a step toward her.

"Fix it," she told him, and he stopped in his tracks. "Fix it now, Zach."

"I'm..." He looked into her eyes and couldn't complete the sentence. He'd been about to tell her he wasn't certain he could fix the device, but the words wouldn't come. "I will," he heard himself say instead, though he knew there was a strong chance it was a lie. He turned from the hope in her eyes, unable to face it and know he might fail. He cleared a spot on the desk where Cody's computer stood, set the device down, then bent to retrieve his tools from his carpetbag. Pulling his spectacles from his shirt pocket, he slipped them on, sat down and began dismantling the small box.

"The pills are gone," Jane whispered.

Zach's head came up.

"They were on the coffee table, by the sofa. But they're gone. Cody must have heard us talking last night...must have heard *me* talking." She closed her eyes. "He's wanted a brother so badly."

"I know."

She paced to the window, parted the curtains to look outside. Then stiffened and turned to him again. "What if he's sick? God, you were so sick when you came through! It will be worse for him... Zach, what if—?"

He shot to his feet and went to her, gripping her shoulders hard. "Stop it."

"Zach, what if we can't get him back? God, what if I've lost him?" Sobs tore through her body, wracking her slender frame, and he pulled her closer. "Damn you and your stupid inventions, Zach Bolton! Damn you for coming here!"

He grimaced at the condemnation in her voice. She was so right. If he hadn't come here... Ah, but what choice had he been given? And yet, even as she railed at him, she pressed closer. "Hold me," she whispered.

"I am holding you."

"I can't feel it."

Zach's arms around her closed tighter, and hers came around his waist, just as desperately, just as forcefully. Her anguish brought his own to the surface, though he'd thought he'd battled it into submission. All the fears that he might not win this skirmish against fate, all the uncertainties, all the doubts, came rushing back, because they were so keenly reflected in her grief.

"I'm his mother," she sobbed. "I'm not supposed to let anything happen to him."

"I know."

"When he's hurt or upset...I can always make it better, Zach. Always. It isn't supposed to be this way."

She lifted her head to search his face, and he pushed the hair out of her eyes. "This is how you felt before you came here, isn't it?"

"Yes, Jane. It's how I still feel."

"I'm sorry...I'm so sorry I tried to stop you.... I was—"

"You were protecting your child. I'd have done the same."

She sniffed, and Zach brushed her tears from her cheeks with the tips of his fingers. "Nothing's changed," she said. "You know that."

She was wrong about that, he thought. Something had changed. He felt it right to the core of his being. But now was not the time to try to understand just what that something was.

"We could still cause unthinkable trouble by trying to alter the past."

"We can't afford to focus on that right now," he told her. "All we can do now is concentrate on getting back there, finding our sons, keeping them safe. The repercussions of our actions..." He shook his head. "Those we'll think about later."

She blinked away fresh tears, looking doubtful.

"And we will, Jane," he told her, and he tried hard to inject certainty into his tone, because he knew just how badly she needed to hear it there. "We'll weigh every move we make before we take action. I promise you that.''

She nodded hard. ''All right.'' Glancing past him, toward the table, where the crippled device lay in pieces, she whispered, ''What can I do to help?''

Seven

Cody picked himself up off the floor and brushed at the knees of his jeans. Then he froze and stared down at his hands. The box! Where was the box? Realizing he must have dropped it, he quickly scanned the room, the floor around and behind him. But there was no sign of it there, and the blinding white hole he'd come through had vanished.

"Oh, no," he muttered. He quickly checked his pockets and found the bottle of pills he'd brought along. Thank goodness he hadn't dropped those, too. He breathed a sigh of relief and, for the first time, examined his surroundings.

His bedroom...or it had been up until a minute ago. Now it was different. And the most noticeable difference was the sickly little boy all tucked into the big bed over there, and the three strangers who stood around him, all of them slowly turning shocked glances on Cody.

Cody cleared his throat, took a single backward step, smiled and said, "Uh...hi." A couple of oil lamps threw off about enough light to see by, and not a drop more. But there was enough to know that those three were none too pleased to see him there.

Moving as one, they came toward him, surrounding him, three stunned faces blinking down at him.

A fat man with gray whiskers, and a taller, skinny man with black ones. Both wore old-fashioned suits and ties. The lady was older, with silvery hair and a crinkly face. She took one look at him and fell backward. Both of the men grabbed hold of her, one fanning her face until she blinked and got herself upright again.

"Don't drop her, Eli. For the love of God, you're dropping her!"

"I'm not dropping her! I have her. For God's sake, get the chair, Wilhelm."

Eli? Wilhelm? Cody stared at the men, too shocked to move. Holy cow, he was standing in the same room with Eli Waterson and Wilhelm Bausch!

One pulled a chair over, tucked it under the lady and then fanned her face. After a moment, her eyes fluttered open, and she smiled weakly at the two men, then gaped at Cody. "Land sakes, child! You nearly frightened me out of my life! What *was* that flash of light? And where on God's earth did you come from?"

"Who are you, boy? How did you get in here?" The younger of the two mustached men leaned forward as he spoke. "Where is Mr. Bolton?"

Cody figured he'd better not say too much. They'd think he was nuts, and God only knew what they did with crazy little boys in the 1890s. So he just shrugged. "I dunno."

"None of that matters, Eli," said the older man. "We really must get this child off the premises in all haste."

"No way," Cody said, crossing his arms. "I came to see Ben, and I'm not leavin' till I do." He craned his neck to see past them, to the boy in the bed. The light wasn't that bright, but Cody didn't think the kid looked very good.

The lady blinked as if she were going to cry, and ran one hand over Cody's hair. He smiled at her, because it had always worked on Grandma Kate. "You dear, sweet child," she said. "Are you a friend of Benjamin's?"

"Yes, ma'am. And I think he'll feel better if I visit him." Cody stuck a hand in his jeans pocket and closed it around the pill bottle. He had to get these three out of here. Get them to leave him alone with the kid for a few minutes, and then he could get the first pill down him.

"Oh, dear," she said.

"Young man," said Wilhelm, hunkering down on his haunches, "I'm sorry to tell you that Benjamin is quite ill. He can't have visitors."

"But I'm already here," Cody countered. "So you might as well just give me a few minutes to—"

"Mrs. Haversham, do you know this child?"

"No," she replied. Then, to Cody, she said, "I know it's hard to understand, but truly, it's for your own good, dear."

"Oh, I understand just fine. You think I'll catch the fever if I go near Ben. But I already had it, a long time ago, so I'm immune. Honest."

The two finest scientists since Louis Pasteur exchanged glances. One pulled his glasses down to the bridge of his nose and peered over the tops of them at Cody. "What does a boy of your age know about contagions and immunity?"

Cody only shrugged.

"How did you get into this bedroom, young man?" the man asked yet again.

"I told you, I came to see Benjamin. Just started trying doors, and here I am."

The other man pursed his lips, shook his head slowly. "And is Mr. Bolton aware of your presence in his home, young man?"

"Sure," Cody said, having a brainstorm.

"Impossible," the man returned, looking pleased with himself. "He's gone into town to fetch the doctor."

"He's gone, all right, but you don't have a clue—"

"Mrs. Haversham, send one of the servants for a constable. We shall find this lad's parents and get to the bottom of this."

"Very well, sir," she said, with a remorseful glance at Cody and a click of her tongue. She moved to the door, opened it. One of the men reached out, as if to grab Cody's arm, but he was quicker than both of them. He ducked the grab, and shot between them, under Mrs. Haversham's beefy arm, and into the hall, straight out to the stairway. They spun around, shouting and chasing after him, but he leaped onto the banister with the ease of practice, slid to the bottom and jumped to the floor. He heard their feet pounding down the stairs, heard one of them saying, "Stop him! He might be carrying the fever!"

Cody raced through the kitchen, and straight out the door.

Zach wasn't so involved in tinkering with the small, dismantled box that he didn't notice Jane. In fact, he came very close to asking her to leave the room. Having her here, so close, made it difficult to stop noticing her, to stop remembering what it had felt like to be…with her. It was the first time in his life a woman had managed to shake him so thoroughly, or to touch him on such a deep level. Or to distract him from his work. Oh, there had been women. God, had there been women. But none had come anywhere close to breaking his concentration this way.

Only Jane.

And his thoughts were anything but lascivious. That he could have understood. But this…this constant glancing over his shoulder at her, with some kind of gut-deep worry gnawing at him…this was beyond his experience. And his understanding. Women had no place in his life, aside from the bedroom. That was the way it had to be for him. He'd made that decision long ago, when selfish, society-conscious Claudia drove a blade into his young heart. But he'd healed. And then he'd enclosed that vulnerable organ within its own custom-made suit of armor, and vowed he would never leave it so exposed again.

And it was a vow he'd kept…until now.

Jane sat with her legs curled beneath her on Cody's bed. Strewn about her were open books, a notepad and a couple of pencils. She'd asked what she might do to help, and he'd suggested she put her penchant for history to use. She was reading all the information she could find on his two colleagues and their development of tryptonine. Once they returned to the past, Zach was hoping, they'd find a way to save both the boys and still not interfere with the subsequent development of the drug.

Meanwhile, Zach tinkered with the device itself. All her information would be utterly useless unless he could repair the damage and make the thing operable. He'd already figured out how to get to the exact point in time where Cody had gone. According to the figures he'd keyed into Cody's computer machine, with two days' worth of recharged power, Cody would have gone back to one day before Zach left the past. He and Jane would try to go back that far, as well, though there might be complications to doing so. He'd worry about that when the time came. He didn't want to allow time for anything to happen to Cody.

He set his mess aside and again scrolled the information he and Cody had spent hours keying into the boy's computer, but wound up sighing in frustration.

Bedsprings creaked, and in a second Jane's hands closed on his shoulders and began massaging him. It startled him that she'd be so kind to him, despite their being of opposing points of view in this crisis. It also confused him. Mainly because her touch brought desire for her rushing back into his loins, and because she smelled so damned good.

"We've been at it for hours," she said. "Time for a short break."

Her voice was hoarse from all the crying she'd done earlier, and Zach experienced another stab of concern for her. She was half out of her mind with worry for her son. He knew. God, how well he knew. Her thumbs pressed into the backs of his shoulders while her fingers kneaded and rubbed the front. He arched his back, closed his eyes. What she was doing felt wonderful.

"It's not the time bending over the worktable that's getting me," he told her as he let his head drop forward. "I'm used to that. It's the frustration."

Her hands stilled. Crying shame, that.

"Then you aren't getting anywhere?"

"Actually, I am. But I know I'd be getting there a lot faster if I were making the most of this...computer of Cody's." He shook his head, frowning at the screen. "I considered myself a genius in my own time," he said. "Now I feel like an ignorant fool."

Her hands began working their magic once more. "You're no fool, Zach."

"No? Even a small child knows more about science today than I. I'm baffled by your televisions and microwaves and aeroplanes. By today's standards, Jane, I'm not fit to graduate primary school."

"You're forgetting one thing," she said, working up and down the back of his neck, and making him curious as to what other magic her hands could perform.

"What's that?" he asked.

"Not even the most accomplished physicist has managed to travel through time, Zach. Not with the help of high-powered computers, or even data gathered from outer space. Yet you did, with tools considered primitive by our standards. You did what they all still believe is impossible."

He turned to look up at her. "I did, at that, didn't I?"

She nodded. "Yes. Which is why I know you're going to find a solution to this disaster." Her eyes were deadly serious. "You have to, Zach. I'm counting on it."

He lowered his eyes. God, but he didn't want to let her down. Having a woman counting on him, believing in him, for any reason, was such an unusual feeling that he wasn't quite sure what to make of it.

"Those circles under your eyes are coming back," she told him. "Look, I'm as eager as you are to solve this thing, but I think you'll work better if you rest for a few minutes. Get something to eat. I think we should stop for a sandwich, and a few minutes to rest our eyes."

He managed to conjure up a gentle smile, and he stroked her hair, something he was growing ridiculously fond of doing. "We're going to get your Cody back, Jane. I promise."

She tried to avert her face before he saw her tears, but didn't quite succeed. He was too astute, or perhaps just too focused on every aspect of her, to miss one so vital. "You must think I'm the most selfish person alive. I was so against all of this when it suited me. And now I'm…"

He surged to his feet, capturing her pretty face between his palms, caressing it with his eyes. "Now you're a mother, Jane. And like any mother, you'll do whatever it takes to protect your child. I don't find that selfish at all…. In fact, it…"

Shaking her head slowly, she whispered, "It what?"

Zach dipped his head, unable to look into her eyes just then. But when he brought his gaze level, he found himself drowning in hers all over again. "It makes you even more beautiful to me, Jane. And no, don't accuse me of using what you refer to as a line. It's true, and every bit as unbelievable to me as it probably seems to you. I've never in my life noticed much about any woman, aside from the way she filled out her bloomers. But with you…" He didn't finish the sentence, didn't even know how, really.

She searched his face. "I hope to God Cody is all right."

"Cody is nothing less than brilliant. With his wit, he'll manage just fine until we get to him."

She nodded. "I know he will."

"So, how about some sandwiches?"

For some reason she couldn't have named, Jane believed every word that smooth-talking ladies' man Zachariah Bolton said. He told her everything would be all right, and heaven help her, she accepted it as gospel. Had she lost her mind?

No. No, that wasn't it at all, she thought as she made a pair of sandwiches and laid them on paper plates. She believed the man because she was fairly certain there wasn't much he set his mind to doing that didn't get done.

That thought niggled at her a little, because it seemed Zach had also set his mind to sweet-talking his way into her heart. Intentionally or not, that was what he was chipping away at, and had been since the day he stepped out of time and into her life. He was…he was mischievous and brilliant, and sexy, and she could fall for him fast and hard. Seemed she hadn't learned as much from the past as she thought she had. Keeping her heart immune to the considerable charms of Zachariah Bolton was a matter of self-preservation. He'd be leaving soon. Very soon. She'd find a way to bring Cody back here, and he'd return to the past and try to cure his own son. And that was where he would stay. In the past. Jane couldn't afford to go forming any attachments to Zach.

But she did have utmost confidence in his ability to pull this off. He'd travelled a hundred years forward in time, she told herself. It stood to reason that he could do just about anything. Rescuing one little boy wouldn't be all that much harder.

Two little boys, she corrected herself with a pang of guilt. Two. Cody, and Benjamin. His son. She'd thought she understood what drove him before, and she'd thought her own practical point of view was the correct one. Now she knew she'd have done the same thing if she was in his shoes and she had the means. Nature couldn't be completely overpowered. Any parent alive would damn the world to save his or her own child. It was simply the way it was.

She opened the cupboard, saw Cody's New York Giants mug, felt her knees try to buckle. But she stiffened them by sheer force of will, blinked her eyes dry. She'd have her Cody back.

Something warm brushed her leg, and she glanced down to see the stray cat, rubbing against her. "I suppose you might as well stay," she said, reaching down to scratch its ears. "You'll be a nice surprise for Cody, when he gets back." She straightened, frowning. Then returned to the cupboards for a couple of cans of tuna and a pair of bowls. She emptied the fish into one bowl and filled the other with water, placing both on the floor. "Just in case I have to leave," she said, stroking the feline's head as it dove into the food with relish.

She opened the back door just slightly, so the cat could get out should the need arise.

"Jane!" Zach bellowed from upstairs. "I have something!"

Gripping a plate in each hand, Jane raced for the stairs.

She half expected to see a wormhole straight out of a science-fiction film hovering in the air in the center of the room. What she saw instead, as she burst through the bedroom door, was Zach bending over the computer, peering through his specs at the screen.

"What is it?" she said, crossing the room and setting one of the plates on the desk in front of him.

"The side effects. I'm almost certain Cody won't suffer from them. Look at this." He pointed at the screen. "I hadn't completed my testing when I came through. Mainly because...I was running out of time. But I had done some, and Cody and I transferred all of the data to this machine. This program he... uh...downfed—"

"Downloaded," Jane corrected him.

"It's amazing. It finds correlations I wouldn't even have thought to look for."

"Break it down for me, Zach. Cut to the chase."

He frowned up at her, but went on. "To put it simply, Jane, the larger the object, the greater the side effects. I suffered pronounced ill effects, but Cody is a lot smaller than I am. If these calculations are correct, then it stands to reason—"

"He isn't sick."

"No. No, I don't think he is."

Jane closed her eyes as every muscle in her body seemed to uncoil in relief. "If he isn't sick, then he'll be fine until we get to him. I know he will."

Zach nodded, but she noticed that his smile was less than sincere. Sadness and worry clouded his eyes. "You're thinking you wish you could be so certain about Benjamin, aren't you?"

"Are you a mind reader, Jane?"

She pushed his plate closer to him, then gently reached up to remove the glasses from his face. "Eat, Zach. Rest your eyes. And tell me about your Benjamin."

He closed his eyes. "If I lose him..."

Her hand cupped his cheek. "You're not going to lose him," she said, repeating his earlier reassuring words to him, almost verbatim. "I promise."

Zach covered her hand with his own and drew it around to his mouth, so that he could press his lips to her palm. "You're a treasure, Jane Fortune."

"Eat," she said.

So he did.

Eight

Cody hid out in a sagging, creaking barn a few miles down the road from his house…er, Zach's house. Whatever. He wasn't sure what had happened to the barn, but he knew it was no longer standing in 1997. And it didn't surprise him. The way the building leaned to one side and drooped in the middle, and the amount of wind managing to find its groaning way through the cracks, were enough to tell him the thing wasn't exactly new, even now. It wasn't ready to fall down around him or anything—he hoped—but the barn was *old*. And if it was old now, in 1897, then it must be *really* old. Maybe even as old as the Revolutionary War. Imagine that!

He didn't have as much time to think about the wonder of it as he would have liked. Later, he told himself. For now, he had something even more important to think about.

The bottle of pills in his pocket jiggled every time he moved, and Cody bit his lip as the sound reminded him sharply of the responsibility he'd taken on. It was a heavy burden weighing on him. But one he wouldn't turn away from. He'd come here to help Benjamin. It was up to him, and only him, to save that little guy's life. And now he couldn't do it, because of those crabby scientists at the house. Was he going to let that stop him? Well, if he did, then the boy he'd already begun to think of as the closest thing to a little brother he would ever have was going to die. Maybe he'd die soon. Maybe he was dying right now.

Cody knew that he was putting his own life at risk by trying to save Benjamin. But he didn't have a doubt that he'd be all right, somehow. Mom was always saying that kids his age believe themselves to be immortal. Maybe she was right. All Cody knew for sure was that helping Ben was the right thing to do. Ben even had the same name as Cody's great grandfather. If that wasn't a sign that he was meant to be part of Cody's family, then he didn't know what was. Benjamin Bolton was going to be Cody's brother. He knew that beyond any doubt, though it made no sense to feel this strongly about it. It wasn't logical or scientific. It was just there, a gut-deep certainty that he couldn't convince himself to doubt. He had to help Benjamin. But how?

Cody closed his eyes and bit his lip. "Mom, what should I do? What should I do?" he whispered into the darkness.

Be smart, Cody. Use your head.

Cody's eyes flashed open, and he looked around him, half expecting to see his pretty mom standing nearby. She wasn't, of course. He was all alone in a big, empty, dark barn, with nothing but the groaning and whistling of the wind in his ears, its cold caress reaching in to chill him through all those cracks, and the musty, sour smell of old hay. Only...he didn't *feel* quite as all alone as he had before..

* * *

It was supposed to have been a brief five-minute rest. When Jane consented to lean back against the headboard, and Zach settled down next to her, barely able to keep his eyes opened, they'd agreed to a quick, short break. Then right back to work. He didn't know when her eyes had fallen closed or how she could have managed to fall asleep at all, as worried as she was about her son. But she had. She'd drifted off as he was talking through his theory about why he was able to move through time. Boring to her, he supposed. If it had occurred to him that he could bore her into getting a bit of rest, he'd have attempted it sooner. The poor woman was on the verge of collapse, her exhaustion more emotional than physical, he knew. And now, though he ought to be working on the device, he simply didn't have the heart to wake her. And if he moved at all, he'd probably do just that. Because timid Jane Fortune was virtually twined around him. A situation he'd fantasized about several times since making the lady's acquaintance, but made come true only once. And once, Zach mused, fell a great deal short of being enough.

He let his eyes roam her relaxed face. A hundred times wouldn't be enough, he realized with a shiver of alarm tickling up his spine. Now what was it about her that made her so attractive to him, that drew him like the lure of the sirens? If only things were different. If only he had the time to find out.

She'd slid lower in the bed, until her head rested in the crook of his neck. Her arms had crept around his waist, and one leg, bent at the knee, held his thigh captive beneath it.

The entire situation worried Zach. Because he wasn't responding the way he normally would. He wasn't sitting here devising seemingly innocent methods of touching her. Or of arousing her enough in her sleep to leave her pliant and willing when she awoke. Though his skills at both tricks were up to the challenge, he felt oddly reluctant to use them. Instead, he found himself content to simply hold her, look at her. Smell her. Feel her warmth seeping into him wherever she touched him. And know that she was getting some much-needed relief from the horror of the nightmare they seemed to be trapped within, together.

He tilted his head as he considered that. Here, wrapped in his arms—in a bed, no less—was a woman he wanted. Quite possibly—no, most certainly—more than he'd ever wanted another. And here he was doing nothing to capitalize on the predicament. It was damned unlike him. Yes, the situation was dire, but he'd never been one to let that interfere before. A bit of physical exertion would do his stress level a world of good, he thought rather sardonically.

Moving very slowly and carefully, he reached for the device, and the screwdriver, and his notes, spreading all of them upon the bed, where they wouldn't interfere with her rest. He grabbed for his spectacles lastly, and perched them on his nose. And then he began to work, reattaching the broken bits to the device, one by one.

Jane sighed, and shifted lower. Her head slipped down to his lap, her hand settling on his hip. Zach pulled his spectacles down onto his nose and peered over the tops of them at her, curled up and sleeping peacefully there, facedown in his... Lord have mercy. If his reaction to *that* didn't wake her, he didn't think anything would.

Something hard was pressing into her cheek. Jane grumbled in her sleep, doubling up her fist to punch the lump out of her pillow and refusing to open her eyes. A hand closed over hers before she could carry out the plan. "Uh-uh, none of that."

"Hmm?" She opened her eyes, lifted her head a little and saw what she'd been lying on. Her eyes widened, and she looked up fast, into a pair of twinkling dark brown eyes. *"Zach."*

"What? You're the one with your face nestled in my..." He let his eyes finish the sentence for him. Then reached out to stroke a gentle hand over her hair, and there was something besides lust in his eyes. Something that made her stomach turn over. "You'll never know how much I wish I had more time, Jane. You'll never, never know...."

She didn't know how to respond to that. So she said nothing. Just held his eyes with hers, and wished she could see what he was thinking. Wished... But wait. What did he mean? He sounded as if... Her gaze darted to the device on the bed beside him. "Zach?"

He nodded, and picked up the black box. "Look at this," he whispered. He pointed the thing, pressed a button, and the tiny pinprick of light appeared in the center of the bedroom.

"My God," she whispered, her heart leaping in her chest. "My God, it's working. You fixed it."

"I think so."

"What do you mean, you think so?" She sat up, got to her feet and took a step closer to the light. "You're not sure?"

"No, I'm not at all sure."

"Then—"

"Wait." He adjusted the dial, and the light grew larger, brighter. Zach got up, gripped her arm and pulled her away as the sphere of illumination took up more and more space in the room. When it extended beyond the ceiling, and through the floor, the light began to take on distinctive shades, and forms hovered on the other side of a swirling mist. The sphere became a mirror, reflecting the room back at them, minus the modern furniture and new wallpaper and electric fixtures. It was the same room, a hundred years ago.

"Look," Zach whispered. "The calendar, there on the wall."

He pointed, and Jane saw the page, with each date methodically crossed off as it passed. "I believe we've done it. We've found the doorway to the exact day before I left. And I'm certain this is where Cody came through."

Jane blinked, shaking her head. "But...but if it's *before* you left, then—then you're there? *And* here? You... There are two of you? Zach, what if—"

"I don't know. I don't know if the past me will be there or not, Jane. I should be all right as long as I don't confront him...er, me." He clasped her shoulders, turned her toward him. "Jane, I have to go now." And, to her surprise, his eyes seemed damp. "Saying goodbye to you...saying goodbye…'' He shook his head, apparently giving up on words. Instead of speaking, he pulled her tight to his chest, and kissed her. He kissed her slowly, tenderly, for a very long time. And Jane found herself kissing him back, slipping her hands up to his shoulders and parting her lips in invitation, and pressing her body tight to his. Before, they'd had passion, desperation, desire. This…this was different. This was emotion…so much emotion that it took her breath away.

Could it be that he…?

He lifted his head away, turning toward the light. Jane gave herself a mental shake, trying desperately to swim her way to the surface of the pool of feeling she'd nearly drowned in just now. She blinked twice, and cleared her throat, but her voice was hoarse all the same. ''I don't know what you're thinking, Bolton, but you can think again. My son is back there. I'm going with you.''

He shook his head. ''The side effects…''

''I'm a little more than half your weight, Zach. I'll be fine. Besides, as you told me earlier, that's not a consideration.''

''It's not safe. Not even necessary. Jane, I'll take care of Cody as if he were my own, you know I will. I love the boy.'' He frowned after he said that, as if the words had surprised him. But then his brow cleared, and he nodded once. ''I love the boy. He'll be safe with me, and as soon as the device recharges, I'll send him back to you.''

''I'm going with you.''

He searched her face, shook his head. ''I can't let you risk it.''

''It isn't your decision.'' Jane pulled from his

strong grip so suddenly that he was taken by surprise. She didn't waste a second, just spun around and ran directly into the light. There was the sensation of being squeezed until she felt like a turtle under a truck tire, and then sudden relief as she hit the floor. Or the floor hit her. Like a two-by-four in the face, swung by a giant.

Zach landed beside her with a crash, and lay there on his side, hands pressed to his head, face twisted in a grimace of anguish. The box hit the floor beside him, and then the light blinked out.

Jane tried to stand, and was surprised when a wave of dizziness washed over her, sending her right back to her knees again. Her brain sloshed as if she'd been drinking too much. Her vision was spotty, and her balance way off kilter. Lord, what a frightening sensation!

But Zach…Zach was still on the floor. He'd rolled onto his back now, and lay there, eyes squeezed tight, palms pressing the sides of his head.

"Zach?" Jane knelt beside him, battling her own reactions, because his were obviously far worse. "Hang on, Zach. Hang on, okay? Zach?"

His eyes opened, focused on her without recognition. Blank. Utterly blank. His brows came together, and he stared at her. "I know you," he said weakly, blinking his vision into focus, and taking in the surroundings. His gaze fell upon the box on the floor, and narrowed as he struggled to sit up. But then he was looking at her again. He reached for her, touched her hair as his eyes probed hers. "I know you," he repeated. "I know your face, and your scent and the taste of your lips. And I know there's no other woman in the world quite like you. Wait…''

"Jane, I'm Jane," she said, but her voice was a bit breathless, in reaction to those words. She gave herself a mental kick. He was confused, disoriented. "Come on, Zach, I need you now."

"Jane," he muttered, lying back down as if for a little nap. She quite understood the feeling. She shared it. Exhaustion. Jet lag to the tenth power. "Come back to bed, Jane."

She took his face between her hands, slapping his cheeks several times. "Zach, come on. Wake up, this is an emergency."

He opened his eyes. "Darling, you're insatiable…."

"Benjamin, Zach. Cody. Remember?"

"Benja—" He blinked, and the dazed expression left his face. "Benjamin. My son!" He sat up, paused to give his head a shake, then gripped her outstretched hand and struggled to his feet. He paused, blinking down at his hand, still surrounding hers. "Jane…yes…" He lifted his gaze to hers. "I'm sorry."

"It's the portal. It does something to your mind, Zach. It isn't your fault."

"We're a day early," he whispered. "Jane, I can't run into…into the other Zach—if he exists. I can't. I've no idea what would happen if I did."

"Well…think, Zach. Where were you at—" she glanced around the room, found the mantel clock and went on "—5:30 p.m., on the night before…"

"The night before my son slipped into a coma?"

Zach finished for her. "I was at his bedside. Nothing could make me leave."

And as he said it, the two of them turned, gazes falling on the tiny, sleeping child in the big bed, and the empty chair beside him. "Well, something apparently made you leave tonight," she whispered.

He staggered away from her, to the bedside, bent over and brushed his lips over his son's forehead. Benjamin slept soundly, not even stirring. And Jane's eyes burned as she moved closer and looked down at his pale face and red curly hair, at the freckles scattered across his nose. Just like Cody.

Zach straightened up, his eyes moist, his jaw taut. "Come on. An earlier version of me is liable to show up at any moment. Help me…" He put his arm around her shoulders, bracing himself against her as if he'd fall down without her help. "Get me to my…your…" He lifted his brows. "Our bedroom. No one will bother us there, and we can plot our next move."

She nodded and helped him into the hall.

Cody waited until it was late enough that he figured everyone would be asleep. And then he went back to the house. He had several advantages, and he'd spent his time listing them, one by one, to build up his confidence. One was that he was a lot smarter than just about anyone else in this century. Nothing to be vain about, just that he came from a more enlightened time. So he ought to be able to outwit every last one of them, right down to Eli Waterson and Wilhelm Bausch. That thought made him smile a little. Imagine outwitting two genius scientists.

Another advantage was that he knew the house like the back of his hand. He'd explored it thoroughly since he and his mom had moved in. And he knew how to get in, even if it was locked up tight. He also knew which room was Ben's. And he had his penlight. Perfect. Advantage number four was that no one was expecting him. So he had the element of surprise on his side.

Now, he also had a couple of things working against him, the main one being that the medication was supposed to be taken over a period of several days, every four hours. If he gave Ben a dose now, and then missed one later, the whole treatment would have to start over, and he only had enough pills to do this once. So there was no way he could leave Ben in that house. He had to get him out of there. And he had to do it tonight.

Cody plotted and planned until the wee hours. And then he gathered up every bit of courage he had, and he tiptoed out of the barn and back to the deserted road.

The road was in worse shape than ever. No hint of pavement, no fresh gravel. Just packed dirt. It wasn't wide enough for two cars to pass safely, and there was only one sign on the whole thing, as far as he could see. A wooden board nailed to a post. Someone had painted Rockwell on the sign, and one end had been sawed off to a point. Cody picked up his pace. He thought that if he squinted until his eyes went out of focus, and didn't pay too much attention to details, it was just like being back home. Only…it truly wasn't. It felt different. Even the air seemed different.

Something clattered and clunked, and Cody went stiff. Then he kicked himself into high gear, and dived into the bushes along the roadside, crouching there and watching the road behind him, as bright as day beneath the moon.

The sounds grew louder, and then the thing making them came into view. A horse, wearing blinders and all kinds of straps. A big black horse, pulling a big, wobbling buggy behind it, and it was headed toward Rockwell. Cody shook his head in stark wonder as the wooden wheels, trimmed in metal, rolled and squeaked past him. The seat inside looked like soft brown velvet, with little buttons all over it. A man and a lady rode on that seat, the lady wearing a striped dress and a hat that almost made Cody laugh out loud. So did the man's long, curled mustache, which was so well waxed it gleamed in the moon's reflection. His bowler hat was almost as good.

Cody bit back his grin and shook his head in wonder. He really had traveled a century into the past, hadn't he? Gosh. It was unbelievable, but he'd done it.

And now he had to do something even harder. Save a little boy who had no hope left except for him.

Unlike Zach, Cody hadn't suffered any ill effects from coming through. He'd had a slight headache that lasted a couple of hours, nothing else.

He felt just fine now. So when the buggy had passed, he clambered right back onto the road, and headed for the house, faster this time. He was getting antsy, and he wanted this over with. There was only one light on, and he knew well enough that it was in Ben's room. He walked around the house, just as quiet as he could, looked around once, and then bent to the hatchway door that led into the cellar. Mom kept this door padlocked, but it seemed like locks weren't as necessary in this past. The door opened, creaked loud, making Cody grate his teeth. Then he ducked inside, lowering the door behind him and pulling out his penlight.

He didn't intend to take time to look around. The place was creepy, anyway. Dark and unfinished. Dirt floor, instead of the cement he was used to. No lights. No washer and dryer in the corner. No boxy metal furnace to keep the place warm. There was a giant hulking iron thing, with an orange-red glow spilling from its every crevice, of which there were many. And a pile of what looked like coal sitting beside it.

Shining his penlight ahead of him, Cody made his way to the stairs, and tiptoed up them. The door at the top had a hook and eye for a lock. It did in his time, anyway. He hoped that was the case here, because if it was he could open it. He'd played around trying to once, when he and some friends played hide and seek down here. At the top of the cellar stairs, Cody listened, heard no one. Then he pulled his library card from his jeans pocket, and slid it into the crack between the door and the frame. Slowly he moved the card upward, and soon he felt the resistance of the hook. He lifted it, jiggled the card a little and smiled when he heard the pinging sound as the hook fell against the door on the other side. Then he turned the knob and pushed the door open.

Pitch-dark in the kitchen. Good thing he knew his

way around. He slipped through, clicking off his pen-light and sticking it back into his pocket. He got through the dining room, too, and then the living room, where he went even more slowly as he approached the stairs. He thought he heard someone moving around up there, but when he went still and quiet, he decided it had only been his imagination.

Silently he moved up the stairs, and turned toward Ben's room. But then he stiffened, because voices were coming from beyond the door. And then footsteps. Cody almost passed out from fear, and then he slipped farther down the hall and ducked into the hall closet.

Jane swallowed hard as she stood silently in the bedroom, staring down at the small, pale-faced little boy. Benjamin, his breathing labored, dark circles ringing his thickly lashed eyes, laid sleeping, his hand clasped in a larger, fleshier one. The woman had fallen asleep in the hard wooden chair beside the bed. Jane could see only the back of her bowed head, her plump, slumped shoulders. And then, as she stood there, wondering how in the world she would handle it when the woman turned and looked at her, she stiffened, straightened in the chair and did just that.

"What—who are you? How did you get—?"

Jane held up a hand to calm the startled woman. "It's all right, Mrs. Haversham. I'm a friend...of Zachariah's. Is he here?"

The woman rose, smoothing her dress's long, rumpled skirts, blinking the sleep haze from her eyes. "No. No, and I've no idea where he's gone."

Jane frowned. Neither she nor Zach had known what to expect. The prospect of meeting another Zach, one who didn't know her, had been so absurd it made her dizzy. "Are you certain? This is very important. I have to know—"

"If Zachariah were here, don't you think he'd be at his son's side? When we've barely been able to pry him from this room long enough to eat or to sleep? No, miss. Zachariah seems to have vanished without a trace, and I'm worried to death about him." The woman's lower lip trembled, and she clutched at her apron, wringing it in her hands.

Jane stepped closer, her throat tightening, and put a hand on the woman's shoulder. "It's all right. It's going to be all right. But I need your help, Mrs. Haversham. I'm looking for my son, Cody. He's missing, and I—"

"Your son?" the woman repeated, and it seemed she calmed considerably. "Young boy...looks enough like Benjamin to be his twin, only older and a good deal healthier?"

"Yes! Then he's here?"

"No, I'm afraid not. He was, of course, but that was earlier, and— Land sakes, the boy never made it home?"

Jane closed her eyes as tears threatened. "No."

"Lord," the woman muttered, shaking her head. "The lad was upset that we couldn't let him see Benjamin. Lit out of here like a bandit, and heaven only knows where he got himself off to. But don't you worry, missy, I'm sure he'll find his way home." Then she tilted her head and frowned at Jane, eyeing her jeans and T-shirt with a puzzled expression.

"And where is your home, if you don't mind my asking?"

"Far away," Jane said. She fought the bitter disappointment that made her want to sink to her knees and cry. She battled the worry over Cody, tried not to let herself panic at the thought of him out there, alone in the night somewhere. She cleared her throat and brought her focus back to the questions that needed to be asked. If there were two Zachariah Boltons running around this house right now, and they happened to run into each other, God only knew what the results might be. "I need to know, ma'am, when did you discover Zach was missing?"

The pale blue eyes welled up with tears. "An hour ago, miss. When I came in to check on Benjamin and saw this chair empty. I knew something was wrong. Zachariah hasn't left his son's side in days, except to go and fetch Doc Baker when things look bad." Her eyes turned pleading. "I searched the house through, but there was no sign of Zachariah anywhere, and no one saw him leave. Please, miss, if you know where he is..."

"I'm here, Mrs. Haversham."

The bedroom door stood open, and Zach stepped through it. Jane gasped as she whirled around and saw him there, uncertain which Zach this man might be. He met her gaze, nodded once. "Hello again, Jane."

Her breath escaped her in a rush, and her muscles seemed to go limp in relief.

"Merciful heavens, Zachariah. I've been frightened to death!"

"I'm sorry I worried you," Zach told the woman.

"But I'm here now. Why don't you go on back to bed? You need your rest, you know."

Mrs. Haversham looked worriedly at Benjamin, who was still sleeping soundly. "I'll go," she said. "But call if you need me."

"Of course I will." Zach hugged the woman briefly, and then she left them. His gaze shifted to his son, and he closed his eyes.

She wanted to go to him, touch him. She wanted to feel his arms around her, and hear his strong, confident voice telling her that Cody would be all right, that they'd find him. But his confident air was nowhere in sight right now. When he looked at his dying child, he was the one who needed comforting.

"Cody?" he asked, not taking his eyes from his son.

"He was here," Jane told him. "But he ran away. Zach, where could he be?"

Zach closed his eyes, moved toward the chair. "I don't know."

He turned as if to sit, but Jane caught his arm and pulled. "No, Zach. You're not going to slip right back into your role of sitting here watching your son fade away. I'm not going to let you. We have to find Cody."

"My son is dying," he muttered, pulling free of her.

"And mine has the drug that will cure him."

He blinked at her as if he'd gone blank for a moment. Gave his head a shake. "You're right." The words came out on a deep sigh. "Of course, you're right."

Jane shook her head, pacing the room. "I don't

get this. We came back here on the day before you left, didn't we? I mean, you seemed so sure. But if that's the case, then why isn't there another you, sitting here? Why—?'' She turned to face him, pushing both hands through her hair. "This is so confusing.''

"It seems to me that it would be physically impossible for a man to exist in two places at the same time. I couldn't be in the room down the hall, and here, in this room, at once. It simply could not happen.''

"Then where did…the other one…go?''

Zach got up and walked to the window, parting the curtains to stare at something outside. "I don't know, Jane. But I do know we came back farther, if only by a day. That's certain.''

Jane came to stand beside him, following his gaze. "How can you be so sure?''

"There was a thunderstorm on the night before I went forward. Lightning struck that barn, the one you can see in the distance. A little after 9:00 p.m.'' He pointed, and she saw the decrepit-looking building. "It burned to the ground within an hour, Jane.''

She bit her lip, nodded. "Okay. All right, then we know we're here a day earlier, and we know the other Zach vaporized or something when we came through.''

"No. I think…I think I somehow merged with him…with me. It's odd, Jane—I remember everything about my trip to the future, but I also remember being here by my son's bedside an hour ago, holding his hand and praying for a miracle.''

A cold shiver worked up Jane's spine.

"Father?''

The weak voice coming from the bed made them both turn quickly. Zach rushed forward and bent over the bed, gathering his son into his arms. "I'm sorry, Benjamin. Did we wake you?"

"No," he said. Jane winced at the thinness of his arms, the whiteness of his skin. "My head hurts. That's what woke me up, I think."

"Well, then, I'll get you something for it," Zach said, standing again, running gentle, soothing hands over his son's head. "And I'll put it in some warm chocolate, since I know how you hate the taste."

The boy smiled and leaned back on the pillows. "I love you, Father."

"And I you, Benjamin. More than you know."

Then those curious green eyes landed on Jane, narrowed briefly, then widened. "Are you her? Are you?"

Jane frowned sending a questioning glance to Zach. He only lifted his brows, shook his head slightly, obviously having no more idea than she did what the boy was talking about. "Am I who, sweetheart?"

"The mother! The one I wished for when I saw the shooting stars! I knew you'd come. Oh, I knew you would. You're just as pretty as I wished you'd be. And—" His words were interrupted by a bout of coughing that racked his reed-thin body.

Jane's heart broke into bits, and she pulled the little boy more upright in the bed, holding him gently and rubbing his back until the spasm eased. And when it did, the little arms encircled her neck. "I'll be a good son, Mother. I promise."

Jane couldn't let him go for a long moment. The

tears that were streaming down her face as she held him there were not anything such a sick little angel needed to see or to be worrying about. Zach saw them, though, and his own eyes were red-rimmed and brimming when they met hers. She held Benjamin in her arms until she could get her tears under control, and then she carefully wiped at her cheeks before straightening away from him.

"You can go and get my cocoa now," he said softly, closing his eyes and lying down. "I'll be fine. I know I will, now."

When Zach nodded at her and inclined his head toward the door, Jane walked slowly away from Benjamin's bedside, and she knew beyond any doubt that there had to be a way to save this child, and hers, too. There had to be. And she'd find it or die trying.

She followed Zach down the stairs and into the kitchen, where he set a kettle on a wood-burning stove, and then chucked a couple of bits of wood on the grate. He stood there for a moment, head bowed, back to her.

And she went to him, compelled to do so. She slipped her arms around his waist from behind, and lowered her head against his back. "We'll make him all right, Zach. I swear to you, we'll make him well again."

He turned and wrapped his arms around her, pulled her tight and lowered his face into her hair. She felt the tears, understood them all too well. "We have to," he whispered.

Nine

Cody waited until he heard the muted footsteps fade. Whoever had been in the room had left, gone down the stairs. Now was his chance. He slipped out of the closet, hurried back down the hallway to Benjamin's room and ducked inside, closing the door behind him.

Benjamin sat up, blinking at him. It looked like he was awfully tired. But he smiled at Cody all the same.

"Hi, Ben," Cody said, coming forward and feeling uncomfortable as all heck. He wasn't sure exactly what to say, how to act. "I'm—"

"My second wish?" The little guy blinked at him.

"Cody Fortune." Cody thrust out a hand, and moved closer to the bed.

Ben looked at Cody's hand, and slowly shook his head. "You better not. I'm sick, you know."

"I know." Cody sat down in the big chair. "But I had it already. You can only catch it once."

"Really?"

"Uh-huh."

"You had it?" Ben sat up a little straighter in the bed. "But you're okay now?"

"Sure."

Ben shook his head slowly. "My dad had it once,

and he got better, too. But...that's almost unheard-of. I heard them say so.''

''They don't know it,'' Cody said, glancing quickly at the door, and then back at the boy in the bed. ''Nobody here knows about it but me, but there's a medicine, and it works.''

Ben closed his eyes. ''I wish it were true,'' he said softly. ''I'm so tired of feeling bad all the time.''

''It is true,'' Cody said, and he fished the small brown bottle of pills from his jeans pocket and held it up. ''This is the stuff, right here. I brought it for you. I tried to get in earlier, but that lady wouldn't let me.''

''They don't let anybody see me, except the doctors and my dad, and Mrs. Haversham, of course. I haven't seen anyone except for grown-ups in weeks.'' He eyed the bottle, and tilted his head. ''My third wish,'' he whispered, then looked at Cody, his eyes round and trusting. ''It really will make me well again?''

''Yeah, but you have to take it right way. Every four hours, Ben, and you can't miss a single pill, or they'll all be wasted.''

Ben blinked, chewed his lip. ''I sleep a lot,'' he said. ''I'd probably sleep right through a dose or two. Maybe if we told the grown-ups—''

''No way. Listen, Ben, they wouldn't believe me. They'd say I was a liar. And there's no way I can sneak in here every four hours to give you a pill. Heck, when I tried to get in before, they threatened to call the boys-in-blue on me.''

''Boys-in-blue?''

''Er...the sheriff.'' Ben frowned and tilted his

head. "Look, Ben, I've been trying to figure this out for a while now, and as far as I can see, there's only one way we can do it."

"How, Cody? I'd do anything to get better again."

"You have to run away," Cody said, deciding not to beat around the bush. Who knew when someone would walk in and haul him away by his earlobe? "Right now, tonight. I found a place where we can hide out. I'll take care of you, and make sure you get the pills on time."

Ben's eyes widened. He took a breath, shook his head. "I don't know, Cody. How long will we have to stay?"

"Just a couple of days," Cody said. "You'll have to take the pills for longer, but after two days you oughta be so much better that they'll have to believe us. At least well enough to take them on your own, without my help."

"If I was that much better, they'd let you stay," Ben said, and Cody thought he was thinking out loud. "My dad will be real worried if I up and leave, though."

"Yeah, but think how happy he'll be when you turn up healthy and strong."

Ben smiled a little. "Yeah, that would be something."

"We have to hurry, Ben. Before someone comes in."

Ben frowned. "I'm not very strong."

"I'll carry you piggyback if I have to. Come on, you'll need some warm clothes. And we'll take a blanket, too." As Cody spoke, he shook out a capsule, then put the cover back on the bottle and stuck it in his pocket. He handed the capsule to Ben. "Better take the first one now. Just wash it down with some water." As he said it, he poured water from the pitcher on the bedside stand, into the glass beside it. He handed the glass to Ben, and the boy obediently popped the pill into his mouth. It took him three tries, and he almost choked on it, but he finally swallowed it. Then he swung his legs over the edge of the bed.

"My clothes are in there." He pointed, and Cody opened the giant wardrobe and pulled out a heavy wool sweater and a pair of pants. Ben dressed, but he was clumsy and slow, and when he was finished he sank onto the bed, head hanging down, breathing hard.

"You really are weak," Cody said. He knelt and pushed a pair of socks onto the younger boy's feet. Then shoved on a pair of odd-looking button-up shoes and went back to the closet for a coat.

"There. You're all set now."

"Take another sweater, Cody," Ben said, lifting his head long enough to speak. "You don't have a coat on. I have one in there that's way too big. It will fit you."

Cody found the sweater Ben was referring to, and then balled up a blanket and tucked it under his arm. "You ready?"

"I guess so," Ben said. He got to his feet, but swayed and almost fell down. Cody moved to his side and pulled Ben's arm around his shoulders.

"Let's go. Don't worry, Ben, this is gonna work."

Ben nodded, and Cody opened the door and led him through the hallway, away from the stairs the other two had descended. He knew the house well, and he knew there was a set of back stairs that led straight to the rear of the house and the back door. It was slow going. Ben could barely walk, but soon they emerged into the chilly, starry night.

Ben leaned on Cody, and took a deep breath. "Gosh, it's been so long since I've been outdoors."

"I bet."

"Where is our hideout, Cody?"

"The barn up the road. I was there earlier, and no one was around. It will be safe, I think. And there are plenty of places to hide if anyone should come snooping."

Ben lifted his head and stared off at the barn in the distance. "I don't think...I can make it that far."

"You have to, Ben. Come on, I know it's hard, but—"

"No, wait," Ben argued. "Listen, I have a pony. In the shed, over there."

Cody looked, and blinked in surprise. There was no shed in the yard in 1997. But one stood there now, right where the garage ought to be. Man, this was like the "Twilight Zone" or something. Nodding, he helped Ben make it across the lawn, eased him onto a bale of hay and opened the shed door.

A soft brown Shetland pony greeted him with a soft nicker and a toss of his shaggy head. Cody gripped the pony's halter and led him outside. And the animal went, stopping beside the hay where Ben sat and nudging the boy with his nose. Big brown eyes seemed to say that he knew exactly what was going on. And the animal stood perfectly still as Cody helped Ben onto his back.

"Good pony," Cody said, taking the halter again and stroking the animal's muzzle.

"His name's Pete," Ben informed him.

"I always wanted a pony."

"Me too," Ben said. "But I've been too sick to ride him for a long time."

"Well, then, you oughta enjoy this." Cody unbunched the blanket and draped it around Ben's shoulders, tying a knot to hold it there. "Hang on, Ben, and holler if you need to stop." He turned and led the pony and the boy across the back lawn and onto the road. Then he started down it toward the barn, and whispered a silent prayer that he wouldn't run into any horse-and-buggy travelers before he got Ben under cover.

Zach opened the door quietly, in case Benjamin had fallen asleep again. It had been a while, by the time he stoked the fire and heated the milk, and melted the chocolate and added the sugar. Nothing like the two-minute hot chocolate from Jane's time. But Ben was used to this. He knew how long hot chocolate took. Zach tiptoed into the room, the teacup brimming with chocolate in his hand. And then he froze, because the oil lamp on the table spilled its light onto an empty bed.

"Benjamin," he called softly, scanning the room as his heart thumped harder in his chest. "Benjamin, where are you?"

Jane came in behind him, and he heard her swift intake of breath. "Zach?"

Zach turned to her, searching her eyes as if looking for an answer, though he knew she had no way of knowing where his son had gone. "He was too weak to get out of that bed," he told her. He set the cup down and dropped to his knees, searching under the bed, seeing nothing.

"Zach, the wardrobe..."

He turned and saw the door of his son's wardrobe hanging open. He pulled it farther, lifting the oil lamp and scanning the inside. "By God, his coat is gone!" Real fear was gripping him now. This made no sense. No sense at all.

Jane's hands came to Zach's shoulders, and he felt the warmth and the comfort of her touch, the calming energies she sent through him as if by magic. "Maybe he just got sick of lying in bed," she whispered, and her soft voice conveyed the same soothing as her hands. "He could have decided to go outside, get some fresh air."

"He could barely walk on his own, Jane." He felt her tense as he got to his feet, turned toward the door.

"Look, I'll search this floor. You go and check all the rooms downstairs. If we don't find him—"

"If we don't find him, I'll lose him," Zach said, and his voice was barely audible for its coarseness.

"You're not going to lose him."

Zach looked down into her warm, wide eyes, and tried very hard to believe her. The panic in his chest seemed to still when she looked at him, spoke to him, when she touched him. Unfortunately, the second he was away from her, searching the ground floor of his home for his dying son, the panic returned. Jane Fortune ought to be pint-size, so he could carry her with him, wear her like a charm around his neck. When she was with him, he could be confident and optimistic, but as soon as she left his side he felt that gut-deep fear he'd been living with for so many months cast its dark shadow over his soul once more. When he'd searched every room without success, he raced outside and began searching the grounds. And when that was done, he searched the guest house, and then the shed.

He stood there, in the shed's open doorway, and a chill night wind buffeted him, tugging his hair into chaos and trying to drive the big wooden door from his hands. Pete, Ben's pony, had vanished, as well. And it seemed all the strength in Zach's body left him as he scanned the horizon, the deserted, dark road unrolling to his left and then the forested hillsides to his right. Ben could be anywhere. He let go of the door, and the wind slammed it back against the wood, then drew it away and slammed it again. It became a rhythm, a hopeless, steady rhythm.

"Hold on, Zachariah," she said, and her voice was strong and firm. "We'll find him. I promise."

That voice was like steel coated with velvet, and it was one he was beginning to think of as belonging to his guardian angel. It came from close to his ear, and Zach managed to pull himself to his feet again. Jane's arms came around him, and he held her the way a drowning man would cling to a bit of driftwood. "His pony's gone. God, Jane, he wasn't strong enough to ride for long. What if he took to the woods? What if he fainted and fell off? He could be lying out there somewhere, alone and afraid."

"I don't think he's alone," she told him, stroking his hair. "I have a feeling he's with Cody."

Zach's head came up sharply, and he stared down

into her eyes. Hope surged in his chest. If Ben was with Cody… "What makes you think that?"

"Well, you just said he was too weak to walk very far on his own. I can't imagine him having the strength to come all the way out here and climb onto that pony's back, can you?"

He blinked, then shook his head. She made it sound so logical, so simple. "No. No, I can't," he said.

"And who else do you suppose would have helped him? Zach, we already know that Cody overheard us arguing about this the other night. That's why he came back here, because he thought we might not. I know my son. He's trying to save Ben, because he thinks he's the only one who can. He took the pills when he left. It's obvious he intended to give them to Benjamin. And that's probably precisely what he's doing, even as we speak."

Zach gazed past her, out into the pitch-black night, and he shivered at another gust of that cold wind. "But that's all conjecture, Jane. You can't know—"

"Call it mother's intuition. I'm ninety-nine percent certain."

Zach closed his eyes. The panic ebbed, now that he had Jane's explanation to cling to. He envisioned Benjamin warm and snug, unafraid because he was in the company of Cody Fortune, already beginning to feel the effects of the drug Cody would, no doubt, have given him by now.

Thank God for Jane.

The wind picked up still-greater force, bringing doubt along with it. "It's so damned cold tonight." Then he opened his eyes again at the sounds of voices coming from the house, and when he looked, he saw the glow of oil lamps in nearly every window. "What's—?"

"I woke Mrs. Haversham, and the other maid. One of them woke the groundskeeper, and he's heading into town to get more help. We'll have a search party formed within the hour, Zach. We'll find them both, no doubt safe and sound somewhere, and probably feeling bad for worrying us all so much."

He sighed involuntarily. "You're a wonder, Jane. An absolute wonder."

She took his arm and drew it around her shoulders as they started back toward the house.

Thunder rumbled in the distance, and the wind held steady, blowing her hair into a riot of silken curls that caressed his face. "Damn," he said. "That storm is moving in already. We have to hurry, Jane— it's going to be a brutal one." He knew, having witnessed its force once already. The thought of his son exposed to such powerful, elemental forces scared the hell out of him. Jane trembled, and he knew she was frightened right to the soul of her for the safety of the two boys, as well. But she wouldn't admit it, would she? Not now, when things were so uncertain.

"We should have thought to bring a lamp." Ben huddled beneath the heavy blanket in his bed of hay. Cody sat close by, but he didn't dare lie down. He had to be awake when it was time for the next dose of Ben's medicine. He wasn't going to let himself fall asleep and miss it. There were only enough pills to do this once, and if he didn't do it right...

Well, he wasn't going to think about that right

now. "We don't need any old lamp," he said, making a conscious effort to sound cheerful. He knew Ben was scared to death right now, and he didn't blame the kid. "Look, I have something even better." Cody pulled the penlight out of his pocket, and clicked it on.

"Wow!" Ben whispered, drawing the word out. "What *is* it?"

"A flashlight," Cody explained, handing his treasure over without hesitation. At least now Ben wasn't lying there listening to that thunderstorm outside and shaking like a leaf.

"How does it work?"

"Electricity," Cody said. "The power is generated by a little battery inside. When it gets light enough out, I'll show you."

"You will?"

"Sure. You can even take it apart, if you want."

Ben smiled broadly for the first time. The flashlight's small glow illuminated his face and his missing front teeth. The pony, who had been munching peacefully on some of their bed, lifted his head and blew through his nostrils.

"Pete's scared of it," Ben said. He played around until he'd switched the light off.

"It's best we don't waste the battery, anyway," Cody told him. "Save it for when we need it."

Ben settled back under the blanket, holding the flashlight to his chest, as if it were a diamond or something.

"Yeah, you'd better get some sleep now."

Thunder crashed, so loud it sounded as if it were in the barn with them. Ben's hand shot out and closed on Cody's arm. "You...won't leave me, will you, Cody?"

"No way," Cody said. "I'm not going anywhere. You know something, Ben? All my life I've been wishing I had a little brother."

"You have?" Ben's voice sounded sleepy, and his grip on Cody's arm relaxed a little, but he didn't let go. "That's funny."

"Why?"

"'Cause I've been wishing I had a *big* brother." Ben rolled onto his side. "Do you have a pocketknife on you, Cody?"

Cody did, but he had a pretty good idea what Ben was thinking, so he didn't say so. "Why?"

"Well, some of the kids, they cut their fingers, and rub them together, and swear an oath, and then they're blood brothers."

"That's what I thought you meant," Cody said, and he chewed his lip, thinking hard. He didn't think it was a very good idea for a kid as sick as Ben was to be cutting himself with a germy old jackknife. "They do that where I come from, too. But some of them do it differently."

"How?"

"Why? You wanna be brothers, Ben?"

Ben looked up at Cody in the darkness. "Yeah. I mean...I do if you do."

"Well, I just told you I'd always wanted a little brother, didn't I?" He could see the white flash of Ben's gap-toothed smile in the night. "So here's how we do it. First, you spit on your palm," Cody instructed. Ben did, and then Cody did the same. "Now we shake hands," Cody said. They groped in the darkness for a moment, but then they connected, and Cody closed his hand tight around Ben's. "And then we say the vow. I, Cody Fortune, do solemnly vow that from this day forward Benjamin Bolton is my very own little brother, and that we'll stick together no matter what." Cody said the words very seriously, making them up as he went along. "Now you say it, Benjamin."

Ben sat up a little. "I, Benjamin Bolton, do solemnly vow that..."

Cody cued him. "From this day forward."

"From this day forward, Cody Fortune is my...my very own big brother. And that we'll stick together...no matter what."

It sounded to Cody as if Ben were choking up a little at the end. And he'd never have admitted it to anyone in the world, but his own throat felt a little tight. "There," he said. "That's all there is to it. We're real, true brothers."

"Honest?"

"Honest. We swore an oath. That's even more than natural-born brothers ever do."

Ben settled deeper into the hay, but he still held Cody's hand. "And you won't leave me?"

"No way. Brothers have to stick together, no matter what, just like we said in the vow. Go to sleep now. I promise, I'll be right here when you wake up."

"Thanks, Cody."

Ben was quiet after that. Soon Cody heard his raspy but steady breathing, and knew he'd fallen asleep. He put his hand into his pocket, closed it around the bottle of pills and squeezed hard. Grating his teeth and closing his eyes tight, he whispered, "You'd better work, you hear me? You'd just better make him well again."

The soggy searchers regrouped at the house. Water dripped from hat brims, and rain slickers glistened in the lamplight as the men filed inside for a cup of coffee and a bit of warmth from the fire. Hours of combing the woods and the ditches along the roadside, and even of canvassing the town, had turned up nothing. No clue as to where the boys might be. And then the storm had unleashed its fury, and the men had gradually worked their way back here, all of them grim-faced and soaked to the bone. None of them ready to give up.

Zach's face was bleak as he listened to one after another of the searchers tell him of their lack of progress. He was soaking-wet, too, and while Mrs. Haversham poured coffee from the metal pot on the cookstove and doled out a cup to each chilled volunteer, Jane took Zach's arm and led him into the living room, urging him into a chair near the roaring fire.

"Just take a minute," she whispered, pressing a hot mug of the steaming brew into his chilled hands. "Here's a dry coat. Come on—"

"There's no time for this," he said, not meeting her eyes. His gaze was riveted to the leaping flames, his attention seemingly focused on the hiss and snap of resin in the hearth.

"You won't do Benjamin any good if you collapse in this rainstorm somewhere. It's only a short break,

Zach. Warm yourself, drink your coffee. Then we'll go right back out."

He drew his gaze away from the flames then, locked it with hers. "By rights, you should be falling apart by now. I know full well you're as afraid for Cody as I am for Ben."

"I'll fall apart later, when they're both safe."

His eyes narrowed as he studied her face. "You're not like any woman I've ever known, Jane Fortune. I know, I'm repeating myself. But I want you to believe it. I mean what I say. You're different from the rest."

She lowered her head. "And you've known a lot of them, haven't you?"

"Dozens."

It hurt to hear him say it out loud, though she'd already known. And she had no idea why the thought of him with all those other women should bother her at all, but... Oh, who was she kidding? Of course she knew why it bothered her.

"Why?" she heard herself ask.

"Why what? Why do I take my pleasure wherever I wish? It's simple, really. A physical need that I assuage when I can. Nothing complicated about it."

"But there are no feelings involved? Not with any of them?"

"No. Not ever. Not until—"

"What about...what about your wife? Benjamin's mother?"

He averted his face very quickly, fast enough that she knew she'd hit on something.

"You loved her, didn't you?"

He cleared his throat. "Claudia, Benjamin's mother, was never my wife."

Jane blinked in surprise, and then in disappointment. God, was he so much like Greg, then? That he'd got a woman pregnant and then...and then...

"She had a husband. An old, impotent, very rich husband. I was young enough and foolish enough to be flattered by her attentions, and to believe she wanted more of me than a pleasant diversion."

Jane tilted her head. "Then...you did love her."

"I thought I did. But I was a flighty youth with more book learning than common sense. I had no money or social standing. She had plenty of both. I was no more than a romp to her. When she found herself with child, Christian woman that she was, she went abroad to visit an aunt, or so the story went. She gave birth with no one in her estimable social circle any the wiser. Even her husband had no clue. The child arrived on my doorstep with a note stating that she never wished to see me or hear from me again, and that if I was to breathe a word suggesting the child was hers, she'd see me ruined. She had enough power to make it a valid threat."

While there was bitterness in his voice, she saw the real hurt in his eyes. "She broke your heart, didn't she, Zach?"

He only shrugged. "It was a painful lesson, but a valuable one. She's been widowed recently. Perhaps being alone will teach her something, as well."

"I don't think she taught you a thing. You became what she was. You closed off your heart and made yourself into a person who's only interested in meaningless flings with strangers." Was that all she had been to him, she wondered? Just one more round of mutual satisfaction between two consenting adults? No, she knew better than to believe that. What had happened between the two of them wasn't based on physical lust, but on emotional turmoil. Shared grief. They'd had no one to turn to except each other, and so they had.

"At least I didn't lock myself away from the world, the way you did, Jane."

"I thought I had," she said softly, and she lifted her face to stare into his eyes and, somehow, swallowed the lump in her throat. "But you got in, all the same."

He blinked up at her, as if she'd shocked him speechless. Then he got to his feet, and set the cup down. His hands rose to settle on her shoulders. "Jane—"

He stopped as the front door was flung open and a dripping-wet, raggedy-looking man stumbled through it. Beyond him, the dark clouds were churning with renewed vigor, as the already horrible storm steadily worsened.

"I seen somethin'!" the man shouted as he swept back the hood of his raincoat. "An odd-lookin' bit of light, in the old Thomas barn."

Zach went utterly rigid, eyes widening. "The old Thomas—" His head swung around, his eyes fixing on the pendulum clock ticking loudly on the mantel. It read 9:08 p.m. "No," he whispered. "Any minute now, that barn is going to—"

A blinding flash split the night, and Zach raced to the door, knocking the man aside as he moved out into the pouring rain. Jane rushed out beside him, and followed his gaze to the old barn, some three miles away. Even as she stared, the tiny tongues of flame began licking up at the black sky from the barn's roof.

"God, no..." Zach whispered.

Jane's calm was shattered. She could no longer hold the mask in place. Her piercing scream shattered the night, and she dropped to her knees in the pounding rain, heedless of the cold, or of the puddle in which she knelt. "Cody!" she sobbed. "God, don't take my baby!"

Ten

Jane's blood turned to ice when she realized that the barn in the distance was the same one Zach had told her about. According to Zach's tale, it would burn to the ground within a frighteningly short period of time. As old and dried-out as the building's wood had seemed when he pointed it out to her earlier, she could understand why. And right now, her son—and Zach's—might very well be inside. Perhaps asleep. Unaware of the danger. Trapped, maybe.

She could only stand in the pouring rain, watching helplessly, as Zach snatched the reins of his dripping-wet horse and leaped onto the startled animal's back. He kicked the horse into a gallop, nearly running an approaching buggy off the narrow road as he passed it. Then he vanished into the blackness of the storm-tossed night.

The buggy rocked to a halt and a woman clambered down, swinging her head around in the direction Zach had taken before hurrying up the steps to the stoop where Jane stood. She was nearly knocked back down them by the rush of searchers surging out of the house as they realized what was happening. Men raced to their horses, and the sound of pounding hooves as they galloped away rivaled the sound of the storm that enveloped them.

"What's going on?" the woman asked. And when Jane didn't reply, she gripped her shoulders, shaking her slightly. The sounds of the horses galloping away slowly faded, until it joined with the howl of the wind and the unending rumble of the thunder. "I asked you what's going on? The entire town is astir. They say the boy is missing, and—" She stopped there, closed her eyes and bit her lower lip.

And for the first time, Jane looked at her. Her blond ringlets hung damply around her face from beneath the hood of the dark blue cloak she wore. She was beautiful. And she was very, very frightened right now. Frightened...and hiding it.

"You're her, aren't you?" Jane whispered. "You're the one...."

The woman's eyes widened, and her lips parted on a soft gasp. "I...I've no idea what you're talking about. I'm simply a concerned neighbor." Her gaze dipped, taking in Jane's wet jeans and T-shirt. "And who in the world are you?"

Jane shook her head. God, no wonder Zach had fallen for this beauty. She had the cheekbones of a goddess. Full, moist lips, and large green eyes that could swallow a person whole. Part of her resented the woman for hurting Zach and abandoning her own child. Another part was insanely jealous. This woman had held Zach's heart in her hands. He'd loved her. Maybe...maybe, deep down inside, he still did. Jane had been trying not to think too deeply about her suspicions, but they flooded into her mind now. He'd loved her. She'd hurt him. He'd never allowed himself to love again. It stood to reason that

that might very well be because he'd never gotten over her.

Part of Jane wanted to tell this woman, this Claudia, what she thought of her. But the largest part of Jane was the mother in her. And that part of her knew and understood the fear in the other woman's eyes. It was a mother's fear for the life of her own child. Even if it was a child she'd never held, never wanted, perhaps never even loved...the biological bond was there, somewhere. Even one as weak as hers must be. It was the mother in Jane that reached out, took the woman's gloved hand. "My son is missing, as well," she said softly. "And we have reason to believe the two boys are in...in that barn." With her free hand, she pointed, and the woman looked.

"But...but it's *burning!*"

Jane choked on a sob, and averted her eyes. "I have to go to my son," she said hoarsely. "Let me take your buggy."

The other woman nodded mutely, turning and starting down the steps beside Jane. "I'm coming with you," she said, sounding dazed.

Jane didn't argue.

Zach drove the horse relentlessly, digging his heels into the beast's flanks even when he knew they were already running at top speed. The road had turned to muck, and still more rain pounded down, making it slick and deadly. Not enough rain to quench those flames, though. He wished he could get the image of that burning barn out of his mind. But he couldn't. He'd stood in his son's bedroom and watched as the flames devoured the entire structure, so quickly it seemed impossible. He knew how little time he had to reach Benjamin and Cody. He knew, and the knowing was killing him.

The wind blew icy droplets that cut his face like razors. He could barely see the muddy road in front of him, and likely wouldn't have seen it even in daylight. His gaze was riveted to that awful light in the distance. The flames spread rapidly across the roof of the structure, reaching to the heavens as if they'd devour the sky itself, and working lower, down the aged, tinder-dry boards. Great pieces of flaming debris fell through the darkness, only to land on the ground and begin licking their way up the sides of the building again.

Zach thought of Benjamin inside. Perhaps just waking to the knowledge that the building was aflame. Perhaps still unaware. Soon he'd be trapped. Soon there would be no escape. Soon...

No!

Zach kicked the horse harder, leaning forward over the sleek, rain-wet neck and feeling the heat that rose from that black hide. "C'mon, Demon. Faster, dammit!"

The horse stretched his legs, lunging even more rapidly than before. Mud and water splashed with every impact of those flying feet, soaking both Zach and the animal. Finally the barn loomed before them like a giant torch illuminating the night and cutting through the blackness of the storm. Rain pounded uselessly down, doing little more than adding a sizzle to the roar of the flames. The horse skidded to a halt and reared up, shrieking in terror. Zach was flung from the animal's back to land hard in the mud. The impact jarred him, but he surged to his feet, heading for the blazing barn even as the horse turned and fled from the terrifying spectacle of it.

Shielding his face with one arm, Zach went closer, until the heat seared his skin right through his clothes, and the roar overwhelmed every other sound. It was deafening. The flames were impassable walls, and he skirted them, circling the inferno as he sought an opening. A way in. There must be one. And at last, eyes stinging from the smoke, he found it. A gap in one side. Like a lopsided ring of fire from some dog-and-pony show. Without a second's hesitation, Zach plunged through the opening, in a desperate dive. He landed rolling in the musty hay inside.

The darkness was relieved only by occasional flashes of flame, springing to life as they found new fuel to feed them. The stench of burning wood and smouldering hay weighted the smoky air, so that it burned his lungs as he got to his feet. He was coughing before he'd gone three steps from the opening. Lifting the lapel of his jacket to his nose and mouth in an effort to filter the air, he shouted, ''Boys! Where are you? Benjamin! Cody!''

He could see nothing but thick, deadly smoke and occasional flashes of firelight. He could hear nothing but the roaring and snapping, which was like a living being. A monster intent on devouring them all. A sudden movement made him spin to the side. Then he was mowed down by Ben's pony as it bolted past him in absolute panic. Zach's head cracked against a beam as he went down, and one shod hoof slammed down on his shin as the frightened animal flew toward the opening. At least the poor thing was headed in the right direction. Gripping a beam to pull himself up again, Zach moved toward the area the pony had been coming from. His shouts and coughing all mingled together.

And then he tripped and fell again. But this time, it was a body that caused him to stumble.

When the buggy bounced to a halt in the mud near the barn, Jane cried out in anguish. She lunged from the seat, jumped to the soupy ground and raced forward, and only the firm hands of one of the searchers kept her from running headlong into the flames. "Easy, missy. Stand back now, and let the men handle this. We're doin' all we can."

She shook her head, and rainwater flew from her hair as she struggled against the hands that held her shoulders. "Let me go! My son is in there! Cody! Cody!"

But there was no give in the man's grip. He held her firm, despite the pouring rain and all her struggles, and she stopped fighting as her knees gave out. She sank to the muddy ground in anguish, sobbing, unable to take her eyes from the fire.

Men had formed a brigade; a crooked line of bodies leading to a nearby stream, where the roiling water reflected the red-orange horror like a mirror. Buckets were filled and passed, hurled on the fire and passed back down. She had no clue where the buckets had come from. Nor did she care.

"This spot. Here, where Zachariah went in!" someone shouted. "Douse this, men, so he can get back out alive!"

Zach was inside? God, all three of them, trapped in that hell of heat and smoke?

In the buggy, the woman who'd driven Jane out here sat stone-still. Paralyzed, in shock, perhaps. She didn't cry out or sob, as Jane was doing. Only sat there, staring, and the light of the fire was reflected in those huge, dazed eyes.

Jane looked at her for just a moment, before her gaze was drawn back to the burning barn that might be devouring her child even as she sat here, safe and helpless. The man holding her eased his grip as she listened for Cody's screams. She didn't hear them.

Then she surged to her feet, free, and raced around the side of the building, slipping in the mud, fighting for footing and then lunging onward. The place the men were soaking in water was a charred oval. Gray smoke spiraled from its blackened edges. And Jane aimed for that opening, with every intention of rushing through it.

A small form stopped her just before she reached the hole. A small, precious, oh-so-familiar shape that stumbled out of the death trap and slammed into her. Small, strong arms snagged her waist, and a grimy face pressed to her belly.

"Cody!" Jane fell to her knees again, in relief this time, sobbing anew, holding him tight.

"Mom...Mom, I was so scared!"

She cradled her son to her, unable to let him go even if she'd wanted to. But her gaze returned to that gaping black hole as she waited, holding her breath.

Seconds ticked by like hours. But finally Zach stumbled through, his son cradled in his arms. Kneeling, Jane stared up into his eyes. And he stared down into hers, his face sooty, his hair singed. He shifted Benjamin to one side, freeing a hand to reach down to Jane. She took it, and Zach pulled her to her feet, turned her and quickly drew her and Cody away from the building. Not stopping until they reached the road.

"Doc Baker!" he shouted. "Someone find the doctor!"

"I'm here, Zachariah. Right here." An elderly man elbowed his way through the crowd and gently took Benjamin from Zach's arms. "I'll see to him, son. There, now. He's alive. He's alive, Zach. Don't go fainting like a woman on me."

"I wasn't planning to."

Doc handed the boy off to someone else. "Get him into my buggy. This one, as well," he said, nodding to Cody.

Cody clung to Jane's hand, hard enough to break the bones, she thought, as he stared at the unconscious younger boy. He turned to Zach, who stood on the other side of her. "Ben's going to be okay," he told Zach. "I've given him two doses already, and in a little while it'll be time for—" As he spoke, Cody dug his hand into the pocket of his jeans. Then he froze, eyes going wide as saucers. "The pills! Oh, no, the pills are gone! They must have fallen out of my pocket when we—"

"Zach, no!" Jane cried, but it was no use. Zach was already bolting back toward the burning barn, leaping through the hole, which was once again ringed in fire.

The doctor swore. Cody cried. The men who surrounded them shouted. But it was too late—Zach was gone.

"Mom…"

Jane shook her head, hugging Cody once more. "I want you to go back to the house with the doctor, Cody."

"But Zach—"

"There's nothing more you can do here, sweetheart. Please. Go with him. You need to get warm and dry, or you'll end up as sick as Benjamin is. Besides, he might need you when he wakes up."

Cody shuddered and stared for a long moment at the blazing barn. "Mom, I don't want Zach to die. I didn't mean for any of this to happen. I only wanted to help Benjamin…." He hugged her hard, clung to her in the pouring rain.

"He's not going to die. I promise. And none of this is your fault, Cody." She bent down and kissed his soot-streaked face. "Please, go, so you'll be safe. Take care of Benjamin. That's what Zach would want you to do."

Cody sniffed and stiffened his spine. "Okay. I'll go. Promise you won't go in after him, Mom."

"I promise."

Cody nodded, hugged her once more, and then climbed into Doc's waiting buggy. Benjamin was lying on the seat, so Cody sat on its edge, and took Ben's hand in his. "You're gonna be all right, Ben," he told him. Doc gave her a nod. "I'll take good care of your boy, ma'am. You see they bring Zachariah along the second they get him out. You hear?"

"I will."

"If I get the lads settled in before you bring him back, I'll return here. Though I sadly fear that if it takes that long, all will be lost." He studied her through narrowed eyes. "What is this 'medicine' the boy lost in there?"

She lowered her chin, shook her head. "I... It's experimental, Doctor. That's really all I know."

"Funny Zachariah didn't mention it to me before," the man muttered, turning to his buggy and climbing aboard. He gave the reins a snap, and the vehicle rolled away. Jane moved forward.

The bucket brigade was going full force again. Two men had gone inside after Zach, and Jane waited, praying silently, as tears slid down her face. "Be all right, Zach," she whispered. "Please, for the love of God, be all right."

There was a crash as the roof gave way. Flaming boards fell to the ground, sending showers of glowing embers into the night. Men jumped back, one of them pulling Jane with him. As the barn caved in on itself, she saw three dim outlines near the opening. And then they were gone.

The sparks whispered to the ground, and the flames that had leaped skyward lowered again, carrying what remained of the building with them. Jane raced forward to where she'd seen the three—or thought she'd seen them—hopping over flaming bits of debris. Two of the men were already struggling to their feet, crying out in pain as they beat their smoldering clothes, and then staggering away. The third remained where he was, half buried in rubble. And Jane went to him, frantically throwing charred wood from his back, burning her hands and not caring.

"Help me!" she screamed, and only then did several others surge forward to finish the job and lift Zach's still body from the mud and rubble. They carried him to the road, laid him on his back there. One bent over him for a moment as Jane joined them there.

Then he straightened, looking at all of them, slowly shaking his head. "It's no use. He's dead."

Eleven

"No!" Jane screamed the word, pushing past the men who surrounded Zach's still body. Her hair was stuck to her face, and dripping wet, her jeans muddy to the knees, her shirt soaked. Her running shoes were caked in mud, and she imagined she looked like some kind of crazy woman to most of them. But she didn't care. "Get out of the way! Let me through!"

"I'm sorry, ma'am. We all cared for him, but it's no use. He's gone."

Jane fell to her knees beside Zach as the rain pummelled her back and shoulders and pounded down on him, rinsing away the mud and soot from his still face, beading on his face and pooling in the corners of his closed eyes. She pressed her fingers to his throat, but felt no pulse. She laid her face against his lips, but felt no breath. Then she slipped one palm beneath his nape, lifting slightly, and she tipped his chin back with her other hand. She pinched his nose and covered his mouth with hers, and she blew air into his lungs.

"Land sakes, woman, you oughtn't be kissing on a dead man thataway!"

"He's gone, ma'am. Best to let him be, now."

She lifted her head briefly, then blew again. And

then again. Someone touched her shoulder, as if to pull her away.

"Leave her alone!" a strong female voice said. And Jane knew it was the woman who'd come here with her. Benjamin's mother. And the tone of anguish in her voice left no doubt in Jane's mind. She still cared for Zach. "Can't you see she's trying to help him?"

Jane ignored all of them and positioned her hands over Zach's chest. Counting silently, she pressed down, once, twice, over and over. Then she breathed into his mouth. And then she pumped again.

"Get her off him!" a man shouted. "It's unnatural, what she's doing!"

Again hands came to her shoulders, tugging her back this time. And again that female voice, the one she knew belonged to the woman Zach had loved, interfered.

"Get your hands off her, or I'll shoot."

Startled, Jane turned, and saw that beautiful, fragile-looking woman, standing there in the firelit night, with rain dripping from her velvet hood, pointing a tiny pistol at the man nearest Jane.

"All of you, back off. Now!"

Slowly the men backed away, shaking their heads and muttering. "She's plumb lost her mind," one man said. "They both have."

Jane didn't waste a second. She bent over Zach again and continued the CPR. She pumped until her arms screamed for relief, and then still longer. "Please, Zach," she muttered. "Please. We need you, dammit."

Finally she felt a soft beat against her hand when

she laid it over his heart. She lowered her head to Zach's chest and dissolved in tears of relief.

Zach drew a raspy breath, then another, and then he coughed. His hands came up, found her head there, and his fingers wound in her hair, holding her to him.

The group of bystanders had gone utterly still. Some crossed themselves, while others swore aloud, and still others only gaped.

"Jane," Zach whispered.

She lifted her head to stare down into his eyes. He licked his lips, tried to swallow. Jane pressed her palms to his cheeks, and kissed him gently, slowly. Her tears dampened his lips, and when she lifted her head away, he licked them again.

"I got them," he rasped. "I got the pills."

She closed her eyes. "I never doubted you would," she told him.

"Let's get him back to the house," someone said, and it seemed the words jerked the others back from their stunned state of confusion.

Jane rose, allowing them to lift Zach bodily.

"Put him in my buggy," Claudia ordered, and the men obeyed her as if they might be quite used to doing so.

Jane followed, climbing in without an invitation. And Claudia came in after her. She took the reins, shook them, and the wheels rolled to life. The buggy bounded and bounced over the muddy road, making sucking sounds and splashing its way back toward the house as the rain pattered down on its top. Jane sat beside Zach, clinging to his hand.

She wondered what on earth she'd done, how

she'd let it happen. She hadn't realized the truth until she was bending over him, realizing he might very well die there in the mud. She'd fallen in love with another man who would leave her alone in the end. A man who thought of women the way he thought of a good meal. Something he enjoyed while he could and then thought no more about. At least…that was the way he thought of most women. With one notable exception, she thought, with a sidelong glance at Claudia. Jane had lowered her guard, somehow, and let a sweet-talking womanizer waltz out of the past and straight into her heart.

And she knew, without a doubt, that when he waltzed back out again, he'd leave nothing behind but shattered bits.

There was something soft petting him like a cherished pet. Over and over it smoothed through his hair, across his face. Slowly, hypnotically. Zach inhaled, half expecting to get a lungful of acrid smoke for his trouble. Instead, though, he breathed the sweetest perfume this side of heaven.

The feminine scent of Jane Fortune.

Jane? Stroking him like *that?*

Very cautiously, Zach opened his eyes, just a crack. Enough to peek out and see her without letting her know he was awake just yet. And what he saw surprised him. She was sitting in a chair beside him—he was, apparently, in his own bed. But she looked so…soft. Vulnerable. There was an ache, a longing, in her eyes, utterly unveiled. No masks right now. Not when she thought no one could see. It was all right there, on her face. And it rocked him, because he'd never seen it quite this clearly before. Probably because she kept it so well hidden.

Tenderness. Caring. Need. And, God, the loneliness.

He turned toward her, reaching out, compelled to do so, before he gave it a second thought. Jane's reaction was to stiffen, and draw away. A mask slammed down over her face in the blink of an eye, hiding that caring, heartsick Jane away behind it. Probably for her own protection, he thought. Dear God, for a moment there, she'd been looking at him as if...

No. That was impossible. Perhaps he'd been hallucinating.

"Jane," he whispered, searching her face even as she averted it and tried to swipe her tears away without him seeing. He smiled at the effort. So he hadn't imagined it, then. "Too late, Jane," he said, though his voice was coarse as tree bark. "I already saw you crying."

"I'm not crying," she told him.

"No. And you haven't been sitting here, touching me and stroking my head, either, have you?"

"Of course not. You're delirious." She got out of the chair, her movements jerky and quick, and poured a glass of water from a pitcher. "Here. You're probably thirsty."

"Thank you, Jane." He took the glass, drank deeply, and watched her watching him. Her eyes focused on his throat as he gulped the water down. When he was finished, he set the glass on the nightstand. He absently licked his lips, and then froze as her eyes flared wider. She quickly looked away as her face went red.

He glanced past her at the window, and was surprised to see no droplets beading the pane. Just darkness, stark and unrelieved. "What time is it?"

"I don't know. Well after midnight, at least." She scanned his puzzled face and went on. "You were unconscious for a few hours, Zach. I think it was a combination of the side effects you were already suffering from and the smoke of that fire."

"I've slept that long?"

Smiling slightly, she nodded.

"And how are the boys?" he went on.

"Cody's okay. Tired, but okay. I set up a cot for him in Benjamin's room. He didn't want to leave him."

Zach shook his head slowly. "That's one special boy you have there, Jane." Then he frowned, and swallowed hard. "And what about Benjamin? How is my son?"

"The same," Jane told him. "I've given him another dose of tryptonine, but it's too soon to see any real improvement yet. Tomorrow, though, he'll start to feel better."

Zach grinned, unable to help himself. "Everything is going to work out. It will—you'll see." She looked doubtful, but Zach couldn't rid himself of the feeling of optimism that had decided to overwhelm him. Not only was his son going to be fine, but Miss Jane Fortune was showing signs of...caring. And that, for some reason, made him feel almost giddy. "And where is everyone now, Jane?"

Her brows rose. "Asleep, of course."

"Of course," he repeated. "Asleep. All except for you. You hold a vigil at my bedside, devoted as a lovesick young wife would be."

"Don't be stupid, Bolton."

"Don't be stubborn, Jane," he replied. "At least admit the truth. Why is it so difficult for you to say it? You care about me, Jane. And you want me, too. Every bit as much as I want you. You know you do. You haven't stopped thinking about what it was like...what it could be like again, if we—"

She lifted her gaze, locked it with his. "Unlike some lower life forms I could name, I do not act on every physical craving."

He smiled at her, sitting up. "You...you'd call it a craving? You *crave* me, Jane?"

"Go to hell, Zach." She whirled to stomp away, but Zach caught her wrist, and slowly drew her back around until she faced him. He pulled her nearer, until her thighs touched the mattress, and then kept pulling, until she had no choice but to sit down on its edge.

He scanned her face, wishing he knew why she denied her feelings so vehemently. "Do you hate me, Jane?" he whispered, searching those blue eyes.

"Of course not."

He couldn't have told it from her tone, or the look in her eyes, though. He lowered his head, suddenly, and began to cough. He coughed until he doubled over, until he fell back against his pillows in exhaustion. Until his skin was coated in a thin sheen of sweat and his lungs felt as though they would burst.

And she was leaning over him, swiping his forehead and neck with a cool cloth, pushing her fingers through his hair. "Zach, easy. Relax. That's it."

Weakly he looked up at her. Now she looked as if she cared again. A second ago she'd looked at him like an assassin. Now her eyes were wide with concern, and her touch was as tender as a lover's. "I don't understand you," he managed to whisper.

"So who said you had to understand me?" She dabbed at his brow again. "Dammit, Zach, are you all right?"

He closed his eyes, nodded.

"I don't believe you. Twice through the damned twilight zone, and then nearly killed in a fire. How much more do you think your body can take?"

He lifted a hand, cupped her nape and drew her closer. Gently he brushed a kiss across her lips, and he knew she didn't object to it when her eyes fell closed. "Climb into this bed with me, Jane, and we'll find out," he whispered, and then pressed his lips to hers again.

Only this time she jerked away so fast she almost yanked him out of the bed and onto the floor. Her eyes flew open wide, and flashed with an anger so hot it nearly seared him. "Damn you, Zachariah Bolton!"

"What?" He blinked in total confusion. What was her problem, anyway?

"I was not one of your one-night stands, that's what! What happened between us..." She balled up the washcloth in her fist, and hurled it at him. "It wasn't just sex—at least it wasn't for me. So stop treating me like one of your giggling sluts, Zach, because it meant something to me. It meant something, even though I didn't want it to. And now I find myself in a place where I said I'd never be again."

He shook his head quickly, scanning her face. "It meant something to me, too, Jane. And what place is it you're talking about, the place you swore you'd never be again?"

She closed her eyes. "Heartbreak, Zach. Its name is heartbreak." Then she spun on her heel and walked slowly away. Leaving Zachariah to wonder where he'd gone wrong. Dammit, didn't she know how he felt about her? How she touched his heart in a way no woman ever had? Hadn't he made that clear to her? He'd never wanted another woman the way he wanted her. Never...never *felt* for another woman the way he felt for her. No, he realized with new-found clarity, not even Claudia.

But then again, Jane Fortune was not any other woman. Far from it, in fact.

He blinked as he considered his unusual feelings for her—the ones she apparently had no clue about—and then he froze, blinking in shock. By God, he hadn't gone and fallen in love with her, had he?

Lord, what if he had?

Well, he supposed there was one way to find out. He'd simply have to sit down and analyze his feelings, the way he would perform any other experiment. Meanwhile, though, enough was enough. He did not deserve her being this angry with him. And he didn't want her living in what she referred to as heartbreak. He'd talk to her. She was going to sit down and explain to him exactly what she was feeling, and she was going to do it now. He got out of the bed, steadied himself, and started for the door. Maybe...maybe he could ask her to stay, after all.... Maybe...

Jane closed Zach's bedroom door and turned from it, only to run smack into Claudia. The woman was the very picture of elegance in her high-necked, lace-trimmed dress. Her blond-gold ringlets framing her delicate face. Her button-up shoes peeking from the frilly hem of her dress. Jane felt like a slob in her filthy jeans and shirt.

Claudia eyed her, then the door through which she'd just come, and then her again, brows lifting this time. "Well," she asked, not even bothering to hide her meaning, "how is he?"

"I thought you were the expert on that, Claudia."

The woman blinked as if in surprise. "You're a very strange woman," she said. "Candid in your speech, foreign in your mannerisms. And your clothes..."

"You have a problem with my clothes?" Jane asked.

"Of course not. I'm not the one who has to wear them."

Jane glared at her.

"Oh, come now, surely we can be friends." Claudia hurried on. "In fact, I feel that I can do you a favor, if you'll let me."

"Oh, really? And just what would that be, Claudia? You going to teach me how to breathe with my waist cinched down to thirteen inches, just so I can impress some male? Sorry. I'm not interested."

Claudia's smile was one of bewilderment, but she

shook her head and went on with the conversation all the same. "I can warn you about Zachariah. Don't fall in love with him, Jane. He'll never care for any woman the way he cares for me. If you pin your hopes on winning his heart, you'll only be disappointed. He'll never give me up for you."

"I'd never ask him to."

"He can't love any woman the way he loves me, Jane. And you already guessed the reason. I'm the mother of his child."

"You're right," Jane whispered. "And I have the feeling you're counting on that, aren't you?"

Claudia blinked, and averted her eyes.

"What's the matter, Claudia? Truth hurt? What the hell are you doing here, anyway? Do you want him back? Is that it? Do you think you can abandon him, break his heart, deny your own child, and then just waltz in one day, wanting to take it all back, just because you've fallen on hard times?"

"Yes!" she cried, and she squeezed her eyes shut tight, and made her small hands into fists on either side of her head. "Yes, that's exactly what I want. Now that my husband is gone, there is nothing to stop me. I need a husband to provide for me, Jane. And I'm not going to let some odd little bird like you stop me."

Jane closed her eyes, shook her head slowly. "Fine," she whispered. "If he's stupid enough to fall for the same bull twice, then he deserves you. But you know, I really don't think he is." She waved a hand toward Zach's door. "Be my guest, Claudia. Knock yourself out." And with that, Jane turned and paced away down the hall, to the room that had been assigned to her. On her way, she opened Benjamin's door to check on the boys. Cody slept in the cot she'd set up for him in Ben's room. Both were sleeping soundly, but she didn't like the sound of Ben's wheezing. Damn, he should be improving at least a little bit by now, shouldn't he?

Well. Maybe in the morning he'd seem better. She pulled the boy's door closed, and as she did, she heard Zach's open. Heard soft footsteps creeping inside, and heard the door close again. Her heart twisted into a hard little knot.

Lifting her chin, Jane moved on to her own room. She left the door open, though, and then tried to tell herself it wasn't so that she could see when the little tramp left Zach's room. Or...if she left.

And then she wished she hadn't. Because after she'd bathed, and dressed in a borrowed nightgown, and brushed her hair, Claudia still hadn't left. And then she lay awake all the rest of the night, twisting and turning and unable to sleep. Because it was dawn, now, and Claudia hadn't come out. Not at all. She'd spent the night where Jane had wanted to. Wrapped up tight in Zachariah Bolton's arms.

Jane wanted to claw the witch's eyes out.

She'd talked herself silly. Talked about all the reasons she'd had for doing what she did to him and Benjamin. Zach hadn't wanted to hear any of it, of course. All he'd wanted to do was get hold of Jane and make her explain herself to him. But Claudia had been insistent and Zach had been weak. So he'd listened to her excuses and her explanations and her apologies. And then her incredibly generous offer to be a wife to him and a mother to Benjamin now that her wealthy husband had died.

Zach had glanced at her, lifted one brow and said simply, "No."

"What?"

"No, Claudia. I don't know how I can put it any plainer than that. I don't want you. Neither does my son. I find it intriguing how you didn't want me when I was poor and had no standing, but now that I'm wealthy and respected, and you're the penniless widow, you've suddenly developed tender feelings for me. As for Benjamin, you've known for months he was dying. You could have spent time with him, if you'd wanted to. But you didn't. Now, when he's reduced to perhaps another day or two of life, you show up. No. We're not interested. Now, please, get out of my room." He yawned, laid his head back on the pillows, closed his eyes.

"It's her, isn't it? That strange woman you brought here from God knows where! It's her. I know it is. You're in love with her, aren't you?"

"Don't be ridiculous," he said softly. But then his eyes popped open and refused to close. All this time, he'd been lying here pondering Jane's feelings for him. God, perhaps he should have been pondering his for her.

"It's true," Claudia whined. "I see it in your eyes when you look at her. And it's even more obvious in hers. The way she stares at you when she thinks no one's looking. The way she touched you when she sat here beside you, the things she whispered. Even her voice changes slightly when she's speaking to you. She's in love with you!"

Zach lay still, staring thoughtfully up at the ceiling. "What an intensely interesting theory," he muttered, and he closed his eyes.

He didn't intend to fall asleep, but he did. With a stupid grin on his face, and an empty feeling in his chest. And when he woke, he was astonished to see Claudia still there. Pacing the floor, peering out of the window, waiting as if for daylight.

"Dammit, woman, what are you still doing here?"

"Leaving," she said very simply. She opened his door, stepped into the hall, and then, for some reason he could not have explained if his life depended on it, she blew him a kiss and said, "I love you, too, darling. Goodbye, for now."

She left, but didn't close the door.

Frowning in confusion, Zach got to his feet and went to do so himself. But he froze when he reached the doorway, because he saw, just two doors down, Jane standing frozen in her own. And the hurt he saw in her eyes was almost more than he could bear.

He opened his mouth, but she spoke first. "I'm glad you're up," she said softly. "Your son has his medication, and you're obviously fine. I think it's time for Cody and me to go…home."

"But—"

"Ten minutes," she said, and her words fell like stones clattering from an unreachable peak. "I'll meet you in the workroom."

Twelve

Zach felt as if she'd slapped him when she closed the bedroom door in his face. Immediately he gripped the knob, shoving the door open again and stomping into the bedroom. She stood with her back to him, near the window. He was encouraged that at least she hadn't locked him out. But then he told himself that might not mean a thing.

"You can't leave, Jane. Not yet." He closed his eyes and congratulated himself on the stupidest argument he'd ever put forth. "What I mean to say is that it's too soon. We don't know yet what... what..." Blinking, he studied her back, her shoulders, the barely noticeable tremor there. The soft, almost inaudible sound of her uneven breathing. He swallowed hard and stepped nearer.

"Go away, Zach," she said, her voice unusually deep and very soft.

He didn't go away. He moved closer, and he clasped her shoulder with one hand to turn her around to face him. She refused to budge. So he tried harder, and he managed to move her this time. Then all he could do was stare down at her damp cheeks in shock. "You're crying," he said, no less astonished than he'd been when he first suspected it. "I can't believe it. You're—"

"I asked you to leave."

"I can't leave." He shook his head, continuing his search of her beautiful face, her glistening eyes. Dear God, had he been blind all along? Could it be true, what Claudia had said? He couldn't believe it. She couldn't be crying for him, or because of what she'd seen just now. She couldn't care that much for him. Could she? "Is it Cody?" he asked her. "Is it all the worry, Jane? Are you homesick?" He touched her face, laid his palm against her cheek and tilted her head so that he could see her better. And when he did, she closed her eyes, as if against her will. And he knew.

"My God," he murmured, taking a startled step away from her. "All this because of Claudia? That's it, isn't it?" She met his eyes, averted hers, and he took another involuntary step backward. He couldn't seem to help himself. It was as if she'd shoved him bodily. The idea that she might...might truly...love him... Frankly, it scared the hell out of him.

She narrowed her eyes. Then her chin fell and she shook her head slowly. "What if it were? It wouldn't matter, would it, Zach? The very thought of it sends you running scared, just like—" She bit her lip, shook her head. "Well, you don't need to panic, Bolton. It's true enough, I fell for the Don Juan routine. You got me into bed. Hell, you even had me believing you might actually..." Lifting her chin, she licked her lips. "Don't worry. I'm taking my son and I'm leaving."

"But I..." He let the protest trail off, unable to find the words, not even sure what it was he wanted to say.

"You see? You can't even tell me you don't want me to go, can you?"

"Dammit, Jane, why are you so angry with me?"

"I'm angry with myself," she whispered, turning from him, pulling her freshly laundered jeans and sweatshirt from the back of the chair. "Hell, I shouldn't be. I ought to be congratulating you, wishing you well. It's a fairy-tale ending, isn't it? You and Benjamin and his mother, finally together. A real family. It's storybook-perfect."

"Dammit, Jane, you think just because she spent the night in my room that I intend to—"

"Don't you pull that love-'em-and-leave-'em routine out of your hat now, Zach. Not now. It's different when you're in love with the woman."

He tilted his head, skimming her from head to toe with his eyes. "Maybe you're right about that."

"And we both know there's only one woman you'll ever love, don't we?"

He turned his gaze inward, frowning hard. "Yes. But I'm only just beginning to realize it."

She swallowed hard. He heard the gulping sound, saw her rapid blinking as she turned away yet again. By God, the woman actually cared for him. It was beyond Zach's ability to understand, but it was obviously true.

"I wish you well, then," she said. "I hope you'll be—"

"Jane," he said softly, again stepping in front of her, tipping her chin up with his forefinger, getting lost in her swimming eyes. "We're going to work this out. I don't know how, but we'll find a way. But first, sweet Jane, you have to know that nothing has—"

"Mom! Zach! Come quick!"

Zach stiffened in surprise, then turned to the doorway, where Cody stood in a nightshirt, breathless and wide-eyed. "What's—"

"It's Ben! Hurry!"

Zach's body went rigid, and utterly immobile. "No," he whispered. "Please, no, not now..."

Jane started to rush past him, but turned when she realized he wasn't following. The anger that had been in her eyes before was utterly gone now. Now there was only compassion. Empathy. She knew exactly what he was feeling right now and, whether he deserved it or not, she cared. Though she fully believed he'd spent the night in the arms of another woman, she could still feel compassion for him.

"Stop it," she told him. And when he only stood there, she stood close to him, gripped his shoulders, shook him slightly. "Stop thinking the worst. Snap out of it. Your son needs you."

He blinked at the strength in her tone, the flash of passion in her eyes. He stiffened his spine, nodded once. Jane turned again, but this time she slipped her hand into his as she did so, drawing him along at her side.

The fear of what he would find when he walked into his son's bedroom gnawed at his stomach like a corrosive. And he knew that if not for the warmth of the small, trembling hand tucked into his own, he'd never be able to put one foot in front of the other. To walk down the hallway, and then to step across the threshold of the open door. With an effort, he settled his gaze on his son. And then his muscles turned limp with relief. Benjamin wasn't dead. He lay there, sleeping peacefully. As peacefully as Zach had ever seen him sleep. But only sleeping. His little chest rose and fell in rhythm.

Sighing in relief, Zach crossed to the bedside, and gathered Benjamin's hand into his own. He closed his eyes and sank into the chair beside the bed, kissing that tiny hand, battling tears of relief.

"Cody, you scared us half to death," Jane was saying. "What were you thinking of, saying that—"

"I can't wake him up, Mom."

Just like that. Five little words, each one hitting Zach in the chest like a bullet. His jaw clenched painfully, and he lifted his head, turned his gaze to lock with Jane's.

Her blue eyes had widened in shock and fear. "I don't understand," she whispered. "The pills were supposed—"

"He hasn't missed a single dose, Mom. I'm sure of it. He should be getting better, not—"

"Benjamin." Zach bent over the bed, gripped the boy's shoulders. "Benjamin, wake up. Wake up now, son."

There was no response. Zach was vaguely aware of Cody moving to the opposite side of the bed, clinging to Benjamin's other hand. And vaguely aware of Jane moving around the bedroom, the sounds of pills rattling as she shook them from the bottle.

And then her voice, sounding dead. "Cody," she said. "Close the door."

Zach looked up, saw Cody frowning at his mother,

but obeying all the same. Then he turned to Jane. "Today...is the day he slips into the coma. But I thought, with the pills, he might..."

She held a capsule, one end in the fingertips of each hand. And as he stared, she twisted, and she pulled, until the thing came apart. She turned the ends, looked inside, shook her head. And when she met Zach's stare, she swallowed hard. "There's nothing inside, Zach. You brought back a drug that hasn't been invented yet. It just...it just doesn't exist in this time."

Zach's stomach knotted, and a feeling of dread slowly chilled every part of his body. "My God...my God, Jane, you were right." And then his gaze turned to Cody. "Dammit, what have I done? What if my coming back here altered history, as you feared it would? Maybe now that I've returned the cure will never be found." Lowering his own son's hand to the bed, Zach walked slowly to Cody, searching his face, fear filling his heart. "How do you feel, son? Are you sick at all? Feverish?" He pressed his palm to Cody's forehead, and heard Jane's pain-filled gasp when she realized what he suspected.

"Just a little tired is all," Cody said. "It's Ben we have to worry about. Why won't he wake up, Zach?"

"Is your throat sore?"

Cody nodded. "Yeah. From all that smoke last night."

Zach's eyes met Jane's over Cody's head. And he knew they were both hoping to God that it was the smoke, and not something far deadlier.

Jane came to her son, slipped her arms around him and slid one hand, very casually, over his forehead. And she felt the heightened warmth of him, just as Zach had. He saw it in her widening eyes, saw the agony, the fear.

"We have to get back to our own time, Zach," Jane said, as she sank to her knees and wrapped her arms around her son. "We have to. And if you want to save your son, you have to come with us. Bring him along."

"And if I'm right? If I've changed the course of things, and my esteemed colleagues didn't find the cure after all? If we return to your time, only to find that the miracle drug known as tryptonine doesn't even exist?"

Jane blinked as moisture filled her eyes at the very possibility of losing her son. Then her gaze turned inward and she gnawed her lower lip. "Bausch and Waterson find the cure because they believe your son died, and that you, their good friend, a brilliant scientist, lost your mind with grief. That's what drives them."

He turned to stare through pooling tears at Benjamin. "He's slipped into a coma now. It won't be much longer before those very things occur."

"You have to make them believe it's *already* occurred."

He swung his head around sharply.

"It's the only way, Zach. You have to convince them all that Benjamin is…is gone. Let them see your grief. And then disappear, never to be seen or heard from again. Everything has to happen exactly as it's supposed to, exactly as it's recorded as having happened in those books I read about you. Don't you see?''

He nodded slowly. ''You're right. It…it might just work.''

''You won't be able to come back here, Zach. Not ever again. You'll be abandoning your work. Your life, your friends. And…and Claudia.''

His brows came together fast as he searched her face in confusion. And then he recalled that she'd somehow come to the conclusion that selfish, grasping Claudia was the love of his life. She must think him a shallow fool. ''Do you think I'd trade my son's life for my own happiness? Even if I really did care for—''

''We're going to have to be very careful,'' she said quickly, and he had no doubt that the interruption was deliberate. ''Plan every single step.'' She sent a worried look to Benjamin's still form, and to Cody, who'd returned to the bed and was whispering to the comatose child, stroking his head. ''And we're going to have to hurry.''

Jane stepped into the hallway and pulled Benjamin's bedroom door closed behind her, just as Mrs. Haversham and the doctor came bustling toward the room. She heard Zach turn the lock behind her. She'd already hustled Cody into Zach's workroom, down the hall. No one knew he was in there, waiting.

Ben was worsening by the minute, and they had no time to lose.

Lifting her chin, drawing a deep breath, she met first one pair of eyes and then the other.

''Benjamin…has passed,'' she told them.

Mrs. Haversham bit her lip, crossed herself. "He's no longer suffering," she said softly. "At peace now, sweet lamb."

"And Zach?" Dr. Baker asked.

Jane lowered her eyes and shook her head. "Not good, Doctor. He's locked himself in with the boy, says he won't let anyone take him."

"Oh, my!" the plump housekeeper gasped.

"I think," Jane added, feeling guilty as hell, but knowing she did what she did to save the child's life. "If we just give him some time alone, to come to grips…"

"Yes, I agree." Doc Baker nodded hard as he spoke. "Let's go downstairs. Leave him be with his boy for a while."

Jane cleared her throat. "Where is Claudia? I think she ought to know."

Mrs. Haversham sniffed. "That one left before anyone was astir this morning. I saw her for just a moment, and she would only say she was off on a cruise to the Continent and to give everyone her goodbyes. Some handsome fellow in a fancy carriage picked her up at the door."

Jane blinked in shock. Had Claudia found herself a bigger fish to sink her hook into? "But she knew…" It was beyond Jane's realm of understanding how a woman could set off on a trip while her own flesh and blood lay sick and dying. But, obviously, Claudia's interests had been in the boy's father, not in her own son. Zach might spend the rest of his life pining away for her, never realizing what a narrow escape he'd had.

She linked arms with the doctor and led them both

down the stairs, knowing Zach needed a bit more time to accomplish what needed to be done. No one else was left upstairs. Just Zach, Benjamin and Cody. Jane's job was distraction. So she brewed some tea, and made plenty of noise. And an hour later, when the groundskeeper returned with Eli Waterson and Wilhelm Bausch, whom he'd fetched at Dr. Baker's suggestion, everyone insisted it was time to go back upstairs. Eli and Wilhelm would be able to talk some sense into Zachariah, they all concurred. Jane hoped to God everything was ready.

Doc rapped gently on the bedroom door. "Zachariah. It's Aaron Baker. It's time to open the door, Zach."

There was, of course, no answer.

"I have your friends here with me, Zachariah. Eli and Wilhelm. They'd like to talk to you."

"Yes, Zach, please, let us in," Eli called.

Doc tried the doorknob and found it unlocked, as planned. He twisted it, pushed it open, stepped inside...and then froze in place. Mrs. Haversham gasped. The bed stood empty, covers thrown back, sheets crinkled and barren. A breeze stirred the curtains in the open bedroom window. The doctor rushed forward to push them aside, and they all saw the rope that hung over the sill.

"By God!" Doc shouted. He leaned out the window, scanning the horizon, but of course he saw no sign of Zach.

"Land sakes, he's taken Benjamin away!" Mrs. Haversham cried.

"Look," Jane said. "There's a note."

Eli Waterson spied the paper on the bed, snatched

it up and read it, shaking his head as he did. "Poor Zachariah. Lord, he's gone out of his mind with grief. Says he's taking the boy into the wilderness, where no one can come for him."

"Lord have mercy, Zachariah's lost his mind," Mrs. Haversham breathed, and she sank onto the bed, hugging herself.

"I've seen it before," said Wilhelm Bausch. "But never in a man as intelligent as Bolton."

"Gentlemen, shouldn't we be forming a search party? Surely we can find Zach and Benjamin...bring them home...?"

"Yes, yes, of course," Dr. Baker said. "I'll see to that. I'll go right now."

"Perhaps you ought to give Mrs. Haversham a...er...a sleeping powder or something," Jane suggested, leaning forward and speaking low. "She's very distraught."

The doctor nodded. "Where is your boy, ma'am? Is he accounted for?"

"Still sleeping. I didn't want to wake him with this awful news, but now I suppose I'll have to. And...well, I'll stay with Mrs. Haversham until she falls asleep, of course, but then I'd like to take my son home. He's going to be terribly upset by all of this."

"That's probably for the best," Doc said. He crossed to the bed and took Mrs. Haversham's arm. "Come with me, dear woman." Jane drew a breath, crossed her fingers and whispered a prayer. This just might work.

Please, God, let it work.

"We'll come along, Dr. Baker," Bausch said,

stomping into the hallway and down the stairs. "If we find him, we might be able to pull Zachariah out of this. The sooner we begin the search, the better."

Zach cradled Benjamin, wrapped in a blanket and all but lifeless. So small, so thin. The illness had ravaged his body until there was little left between his skin and his bones. His drawn face lay still and quiet. Pale as a wraith, except for the purplish wells that housed his eyes. Cody sat nearby, steadfast and quiet. But Zach knew full well it was all the child could do to contain his tears. He was trying, valiantly, to behave the way he thought a man should behave. And doing a sight better at it at the ripe old age of ten than Zach was doing at thirty-five.

There was a tap at the workroom door that brought Zach's head up sharply. He sat still, silent, and held one hand up to tell Cody to do the same. He needn't have. The boy knew the plan as well as he did. After a brief pause, there were two more knocks on the door. Zach nodded at Cody, and the boy crossed the room to unlock it.

Jane came inside, looking slightly ill. Lying about the death of an innocent child, he supposed, wasn't likely to have agreed with her. She was nothing if not honest. Brutally so, at times.

And strong, he mused as she stepped quietly inside, closing the door behind her. Strong, when he so needed strength. He'd never have expected to find a wellspring of it embodied in one petite female. Looks, he decided, could certainly be deceiving.

"It's done," she said softly.

"We're alone in the house?"

"Doc's gone into town to form a search party. Bausch and Waterson are with him. I made him give Mrs. Haversham a sedative before he left, and she's sound asleep now."

"Good. Let's get on with this, then, before someone else shows up." He stood, cradling Ben in his arms, and they all walked into the hallway, and down it, to Benjamin's room. Jane kept one arm around Cody, and closed the door after they entered.

Zach didn't waste any time. He laid Benjamin carefully on his bed. Then he took the little black box from his pocket, pointed it toward the room's center. "Are you ready?"

Jane nodded firmly. "The question is, are you? You're giving up an awful lot, Zach."

He scowled at her and flicked the button. Immediately the pinprick of light appeared in the room's center. Zach turned the dial slowly, and the light grew bigger and brighter. Silvery mists swirled like a tempest inside, then gradually cleared until the sphere shone like a mirror, reflecting the room back at them...from a hundred years into the future.

"You're going to be sick again, Zach."

"But my son will be well," he said. He tucked the device firmly into his pocket, then gathered Benjamin into his arms again. "Jane?" Shifting Benjamin to one side, he reached for Jane's hand with his free one.

She took it, pulling Cody tight to her other side.

Zach stepped through the glimmering doorway, and the impact this time was more like being hit by a truck than a post.

Thirteen

As she pulled herself to her feet, Jane battled dizziness and terrible nausea. She gripped the foot of Cody's bed to keep from falling to her knees again, then paused and blinked at it. Cody's bed. And beside it was Cody's desk, and his computer, and his stack of books.

She turned quickly, and saw her son, picking himself up off the floor and looking a little stunned. And then her gaze found Zach, lying still, his arms wrapped tightly around Benjamin, who wasn't stirring a bit. Staggering a little, she went to them, knelt beside their embracing forms.

"Zach? Zach, are you all right?"

His eyes blinked open when she touched his face. His lips moved, but no words came out. Very gently, she eased his arms from around his son, and gathered Benjamin into her own. She heard his slow, labored breathing as she carried him to Cody's bed and carefully laid him down.

"He oughta be in a hospital, Mom."

She nodded, turning to Cody. "You're right, as usual, kiddo. How about you? Are you okay?"

"That time traveling packs one heck of a wallop, but yeah, I'm okay." He frowned up at her, seeming

older than he had any right to. "You don't look so
good, though."

She waved a dismissive hand at him. "What about
your sore throat?"

Cody tilted his head, ran his fingertips over his
Adam's apple. "That's odd."

"What, honey?" Jane would have sworn every
cell in her body froze as she awaited his answer.

"It's gone."

"Gone," she whispered, closing her eyes. She
nearly went limp with relief, hoping, praying, that
this meant what she thought it did. She touched
Cody's forehead, laid her palm on his cheek, but he
didn't seem feverish now, though he had only seconds ago. Please, she thought, please let it be okay.

"Mom, we'd better hurry. You want me to call an
ambulance?"

"What? Oh, yes, I guess you'd better."

Cody raced from the room, and she heard his feet
pounding down the stairs to the only telephone in the
house. Jane bent over Benjamin, stroked his hair
away from his face. "You hold on a bit longer, little
one. We're going to take care of you. I promise."

"Jane?"

She turned at the strained sound of Zach's voice.
He'd pulled himself into a sitting position, one palm
pressed to his forehead, eyes squeezed tight. She
went to him, knelt beside him. "It's all right, Zach.
We made it back, and there's an ambulance on the
way."

He lifted his head, searched her eyes. "Benjamin?"

"He's hanging in there."

He brought one hand up to cup her face, stared into her eyes. "And you, Jane? What about you?"

My heart's breaking, you idiot.

"I'm fine."

But she wasn't. All along, she'd resisted her feelings for Zach, because she'd known he'd leave her in the end, to return to his own time, a century in the past. Now he was here to stay. But his heart remained back there, with a woman who wasn't even worthy of a passing glance from a man like him. She'd been foolish, but there was no help for it. She'd gone and let herself fall in love with the jerk.

"Then..." His thumb brushed across her cheek, "Why are there tears in your eyes?"

She tried to blink the alleged tears away. "When the ambulance arrives, Zach, you ought to let them take you to the hospital, too."

"I'll go, Jane, but not as a patient. I need to be with my son."

She nodded, understanding that perfectly. "What if you have another memory lapse, like last time?"

"You'll be with me...won't you, Jane?" His eyes probed hers so deeply she felt their touch on her very soul.

"Of course I will."

He smiled weakly. "Good. If my memory does fail me again, you'll be able to handle it. I have no doubt about that."

"That's me," she whispered. "Solid, dependable Jane."

Zach frowned, and tilted his head. "And just what is that supposed to mean?"

"Nothing. Nothing at all."

* * *

Jane said her head felt a little clearer by the time the ambulance—a motorcar painted white, with flashing lights and a screaming noise to it—arrived. So she and Cody followed in her auto. Zach climbed into the back of the noisy machine to ride with his son, all the while answering the questions of the fellow who rode back there with him.

"Any history of allergies?"

"Uh…no. But he hasn't been exposed to much in the way of modern drugs." The man looked at Zach strangely. "We've been living in remote areas, in, uh, India." He hoped to God there were still remote areas in India.

"I see. So, is he up-to-date on his immunizations?"

"Probably not," Zach confessed, and he winced as a needle with a rubberized tube attached was inserted into his son's forearm. "What's that?"

"Just fluids. We get the IV started now, and it'll be easier to administer whatever drugs he needs at the hospital."

Zach studied the tubing, and the liquid-filled bag attached. Ringers Lactate, it read. "Ingenious."

"And what makes you think this is quinaria fever?"

Zach blinked, hoping he was giving all the right answers. If ever he'd needed Jane by his side, it was now. Then again, it seemed he felt that way whenever he was away from her. He didn't just need her now, but always. "He was exposed," he said to the attendant. "There was an outbreak in the village where we were staying."

"Damn. I thought that disease was pretty well eradicated by now."

"Then...then there is a cure?"

The younger man looked at Zach as if he were insane. "Man, that must have been one isolated village. There's been a cure for almost a hundred years now. Don't know how you could spend a day in Rockwell and not know about it. It's our town's one and only claim to fame."

He kept on talking while he worked on Benjamin, and Zach listened, bouncing with the rhythm of the speeding vehicle as it raced toward the hospital, to the story of Zachariah Bolton, the brilliant scientist who'd lost his mind with grief at the death of his son. And of his two colleagues, who'd joined forces to develop a cure, in honor of their lost friend.

Zach couldn't stop the tears of relief that flowed unchecked as he heard the tale, unchanged from the way Jane had told it to him only a few days ago. *Unchanged.* And the medic only looked at him oddly as he closed his eyes and whispered, "It worked, Jane. We did it."

The young man's hand fell onto Zach's shoulder. "If he makes it to the hospital, pal, they'll be able to pull him through. You hang tough, okay?"

Jane sipped the stale, machine-generated coffee, grimaced and set it on the vinyl table beside the vinyl chair in which she sat. Cody had fallen asleep in the seat beside her. Zach was still pacing. He hadn't stopped since they'd arrived here, in time to see him being firmly told he had to stay in the waiting room while Benjamin was being treated. He'd argued, naturally. It wasn't like Zach to give up without a fight. Jane had intervened, though, guiding him to this bustling waiting area, and he'd been pacing ever since. The fear and worry on his face were more than she could stand.

She got up, took his hand. "Sit down, Zach. You're exhausted, and dizzy, and all this pacing isn't going to do Benjamin any good."

He stopped walking, but didn't sit. He just stared down at her, gripping her hand tightly. "What if he doesn't make it, Jane? What if—?"

"He'll make it. He can't give up now, not after all we've gone through. I can't believe we made it this far only to lose him, Zach. I won't believe it."

"It's been so long. Two hours now." Zach turned toward the double doors with the mesh-lined windows. "I have to know what's happening in there."

"Zach—"

He pulled free of her restraining hand, and headed for the doors. But before he reached them, Dr. Mulligan emerged and held up his hands. Zach came to a wobbly stop, and Jane hurried up beside him. She slid her arm around his waist, since he was none too steady on his feet.

"How is my son?" His voice, when he said it, was little more than a coarse whisper.

"We've stabilized him."

"Then he's all right?"

"Not yet. He's still in a coma, but we've started an IV with tryptonine. Once the drug begins to take effect, we're hoping he'll come around."

"Hoping?"

"Mr...." The doctor paused, glanced down at the

chart in his hands and looked up at Zach again. "Bolton," he went on. "We can't be sure of anything at this point. If your son can hold on long enough for the medicine to take effect, we'll be able to pull him through, but there's still a great chance that he won't. I have to be honest with you about that. You should prepare yourself."

Jane felt the jolt that went through Zach's body, and she held him tighter. His arm came around her shoulders, as if he were clinging to her for survival. "Go on," he said, when he could speak again.

The doctor lowered his head. "Even if he survives, there's a possibility of brain damage. His fever was very high when he was brought in. We have no way of knowing how, or even if, that affected him. We'll only know when he comes around. He might be just fine, Mr. Bolton. But there's a slim chance his motor skills and cognitive abilities could be impaired for the rest of his life. We just can't tell at this point."

"I see."

"We should know something by morning."

Zach nodded. Then as the doctor turned to go, he brought his head up sharply. "Can I see him?"

"Of course. We'll be moving him to his room shortly, so you'll have to keep it brief."

Zach started forward, his arm still anchored around Jane.

"Only family," the doctor said softly.

"Jane *is* family," Zach replied, and kept right on going.

"Go home, Jane. You need rest."

She didn't, though. She came the rest of the way

into the stark white room, with its wondrous beeping and blinking machines. She came all the way to the chair where Zach had been sitting for what seemed like years, and she gently took his son's limp hand from his much larger one, enclosing it lovingly in her own. "I've been home. I brought you a change of clothes and something to eat," she said softly, her gaze pinned to the face of his son.

She smelled good. Fresh and clean. She'd changed clothes herself, though it didn't look to Zach as if she'd taken the time to get any sleep. Knowing Jane, he'd say she'd rushed home and back for his sake more than her own. She laid Benjamin's hand down atop the bedsheet, and then opened the small bag that hung from her shoulder. She pulled a container from it, and then a plastic-wrapped spoon. "Here. Yogurt. It's good for you. I've got some cookies, and a few—"

"Where is Cody? Not still sleeping on that horrendous excuse for a chair in the waiting room, I hope."

Smiling slightly, Jane shook her head. "A nurse took pity and let me lay him in a vacant bed in the next room. I just hope I don't get billed for it."

She said it in jest, he knew, but the thought of bills and such made him wince. He'd been a man of means in his time. Now...now he had no clue how he'd begin to make his way. But he couldn't worry over that now. He couldn't think of anything else, except his son, lying here in this strange bed, perhaps at the brink of...

"Father?"

The yogurt cup fell to the floor from nerveless

fingers as Zach's heart swelled to bursting. Eyes wide, he turned his head slowly. But Benjamin wasn't focused on him. Instead, he was blinking up at Jane, as if he were seeing an angel. She stroked his hair away from his forehead and leaned low to place a tender kiss there. Then she stepped away, making room for Zach at his son's bedside.

"Benjamin," he whispered, tears choking him. Ben tried to sit up, lifting his arms to his father, and Zach responded by wrapping his arms around his son's thin frame and holding him very close. "You're awake. Thank God, my son, you're awake." His words deteriorated to grateful mutters as he buried his face in his son's red curls and closed his eyes to hide his tears.

"It was Cody's medicine, Father. He said it would make me well again, and..." Ben backed up a little, staring up at his father. "Is it true? Am I really going to be well, Father?"

Stroking those riotous curls, Zach nodded. "It's true."

"It was my wish, you know. The shooting stars... I knew it wasn't very scientific, Father, but when I saw them from my bedroom window, I wished on them. And my wishes came true. All three of them really came true!" He lay back on the pillows, sighing, and Zach knew he was still easily tired. But, by God, there were healthy splashes of color in his cheeks now. And his eyes had regained some of their former shine.

"Three wishes?"

"Oh, yes! My first wish was to be well again. That came true. And then I wished for a big brother, and

Cody came. He promised he'd be..." Benjamin blinked and looked around the room, and Zach did the same. "But...he didn't leave me, did he?"

"No, son. Cody is taking a nap in the next room." And, apparently, his mother had decided to join him there. She must have slipped out to give him time alone with his son.

"Oh." Benjamin frowned, tilting his head. "We're not home, are we, Father?"

"No, son, we're in a hospital, a long ways from home."

Squinting at the overhead light fixture, Benjamin said, "We must be where Cody comes from, huh?"

Now how in the world could he know that? No matter. "Tell me about the rest of your wishes, Benjamin. What else did you wish for? Whatever it is, I'll get it for you, I swear."

Benjamin grinned, and Zach fully expected to hear a request for a new toy or a puppy or some such. Instead, he heard, "Oh...well, like I said, I wished for a big brother. I've been wanting one for ever so long, Father. But you don't need to get one for me. Cody is my brother now."

"He is?"

"Uh-huh. We swore an oath. Those were my first two wishes, and they both came true. And there's only one more to go. And I think it's come true, too."

Swallowing hard, Zach whispered, "What's the third wish, Ben?"

"I want a mother," Benjamin whispered, closing his eyes and smiling softly. "I want a real mother, who will live with us and who will love me for always.'' He tilted his head, and looked at his father. ''I know you've been looking for one for a long time, Father, but you never find any really good ones. Anyway, it doesn't matter now, because I have her all picked out.''

''You do, do you?''

Benjamin nodded firmly, then looked toward the door, his eyes lighting up. Jane stood there, and Zach was left with no doubt about the identity of the woman his son had chosen. And then Cody crowded past her, and raced to the opposite side of the bed. The two boys chattered excitedly, seemingly forgetting the presence of the adults in the room. Jane took Zach's arm and gently led him into the hallway.

''You look worried. Zach, you ought to be relieved. He looks so much better.''

Searching her face, Zach saw the telltale traces of tearstains. ''I'll never get over how deeply you feel things, Jane Fortune,'' he whispered, tracing those marks on her cheeks with his fingertips.

''What is it you're worrying about?'' she persisted.

He shook his head. ''A hundred things. A thousand. My son is well, though, so what right do I have to complain? I'd live in the streets and be happy.''

''Is that it? You're wondering where you'll live when he's released? Zach, you know you're welcome to stay with Cody and me for as long as—''

Shaking his head, Zach turned away from her. ''And how long would that be, Jane? How long do you suppose it will take a man like me to find a means to earn a living in this time? I don't even know where to begin.''

She placed a hand on his shoulder. "Zach, you're a genius."

"No. I was a genius. Surrounded by modern technology, I'm a bumbling fool." He sighed hard, and began to pace. "I'm back where I began. A man with little wealth and no social standing. No security. Nothing to offer a woman—" He bit his lip, and broke off.

"A woman?" Jane repeated. "Zach, I know you miss Claudia, but you can't possibly be thinking of going back there and bringing her—"

"Can't that brain of yours think about anything but Claudia?" he snapped. She blinked hard at his harsh tone, and Zach instantly regretted it. But the woman was so frustrating! Ah, but who did he have to blame for her misconceptions? No one but himself. "I'm simply trying to illustrate how ill-equipped I am to make a living for myself, much less anyone else, amid the modern technology of today's society." He hoped that covered his slip, as well as his bad manners. He was too tired to think this through right now, and too frustrated to be this close to her without touching her. He recalled her telling him that her family was one of the wealthiest in the country. Good God, he felt as if he'd gone backward in time all over again.

"Modern technology, my foot," she snapped, and then she spun him around to face her, with more force than he'd expected. "You traveled through time, Zachariah Bolton. No other scientist has managed to do that, not with the help of every scrap of modern technology available today. Not one. You're still a genius. And you'll find a way to apply that brain of yours in today's world. I know you will.''

He swallowed hard, but nodded. ''Perhaps...''

''I'll help you,'' she told him. And he knew perfectly well she meant it.

''Why, Jane?'' he whispered. ''Why are you so good to me?''

Lowering her chin, she shook her head slowly. ''We've been through hell together, Zach. I...like to think we're...friends. And besides, you'd do the same for me.''

I'd cut out my heart for you, he wanted to tell her. But, of course, he couldn't. Not now. Especially not now. In fact, maybe it was better that she go on believing he was pining away for selfish little Claudia.

It wasn't what he wanted her to think. Not at all. He wanted to tell her...to tell her that he had done what he'd never in his life believed himself capable of doing. That he'd fallen in love with her. He wanted...good God, he wanted to ask Jane Fortune to marry him. Ben loved her. And, dammit, so did he.

But how could he ask that of her? He knew she was trying to get by without her fortune, but it was there, all the same. It was there. And what would she want with a man who was only steps away from being a pauper? She couldn't be expected to continue giving to him and Ben. He couldn't ask it of her. Nor of himself.

He looked at her, everything in him aching to tell her that it was her he loved, not Claudia. But instead, he clamped his jaw, and said nothing.

Fourteen

Dammit, why did men have to be such utter fools? She'd had it with them. Or… Well, she'd thought she'd had it with them. Until now. Now she'd made up her mind that no man would ever figure anything out unless a woman drew him a picture. Oh, she had her pride. And pride was all well and good, but facts were facts. And the fact was that more than her heart would be broken when Zachariah Bolton marched out of her life. Cody would be shattered, as well. He loved Zach madly, and had claimed little Benjamin as his very own brother. It would kill him to lose those two. And Benjamin was just as enamored of Cody. Not only that, but the boy seemed to have become attached to her. And, God, how she had fallen in love with that little tyke. Those carrot curls and those big blue eyes and that mischievous grin. He'd been home from the hospital for a week now, and he'd dug himself a permanent place in Jane's heart. She loved him so much she felt as if she'd given birth to him. And she was not going to let him go. Not without a fight.

That damn thickheaded Zachariah Bolton had been brooding for days, heartsick, no doubt, over losing the selfish little witch he'd fancied himself in love with. And when he wasn't moon-eyed over his lost love, he was scheming and plotting ways to earn a decent living in the 1990's. There was no doubt whatsoever in Jane's mind that the second he got his hands on a dependable income, he'd take his son and march straight out of her life. Which was why she hadn't told him what she'd discovered when she finally got into that old safe that was stored in the attic. If she told him, she'd lose him. She'd been waiting, hoping against hope that he'd realize he belonged with her. Maybe even begin to love her a little bit.

But the jerk hadn't come around, even after a week, and she was beginning to think he never would. Time to change tactics.

Besides, she couldn't keep the information from him much longer. But she'd made up her mind that when she told him about that, she was going to tell him everything else, as well. Might as well lay it on the line and go for broke. Her delaying tactics certainly hadn't been effective.

So she was going to tell him, flat out, tonight. She'd had all she could stand of watching him pine for another woman, and not even notice her. Enough was enough. More than enough, thank you very much.

It was driving him insane, living with her! Dammit, she seemed to go out of her way to be near him, tormenting him with her presence until he thought he'd go mad with wanting her. Must she wear those formfitting jeans all the time? Must she always leave her hair loose and flowing, for God's sake? Couldn't she bundle it up, spinster-style, just once? And for the love of God, why did she have to *smell* so good?

Why did she have to sing in the shower? Why did she have to be so blasted loving and caring to his son that it melted his heart each time he saw it. Why?

He wanted her. Not just in his bed, but right to the base of his soul, he wanted her. He'd thought he'd loved once, but with every day that passed, he realized more and more how dim his young yearnings for Claudia had been in comparison with the real thing. But he hadn't told Jane. He had his pride, dammit, and right now he had nothing to offer her. Nothing at all. He'd been slowly growing more and more frustrated as he sought to find his place in this new world, to understand where he fit in, to find a way to earn a living, for heaven's sake. But he hadn't. Not yet.

But he would. He'd find his way and he'd make Jane his own. It was the waiting that was driving him to distraction.

"Zachariah?"

He turned to see the object of his every waking thought, standing in the doorway of his workroom. He caught her unaware, and in that instant before she felt his gaze, he saw her pain, etched into the porcelain features of her face. Pain he'd caused. Hell, she cared for him. And he'd been a fool to let her go on believing he didn't feel the same. In that moment, he changed his mind. He couldn't wait any longer. To hell with his pride. To hell with his income, or lack thereof. He'd deal with that later. It was important, yes, but not as important as what he felt for this woman. Nothing was as important as that.

Jane had moved Cody to another bedroom, worried about prolonged exposure to the time warp that existed, invisible, here in this one. Benjamin had the room beside Cody's, though they spent most of their time together in one place or the other. Usually wherever the Nintendo machine was set up at the time. Zach had set up a cot in here.

Jane was not smiling when she met his eyes. Lord, he'd done something to make her angry. Well, he deserved her anger for allowing her to doubt him so long. And he couldn't blame her, could he?

"We have to talk," she said.

"Yes, we do," he said. "It's long overdue."

"Not here. I don't want to wake the boys. Downstairs, okay?" And without another word, she backed out into the hall, closing the door behind her.

Zach drew a fortifying breath, and got to his feet, closing the journal where he'd been recording his thoughts. Jane had suggested he try his hand at writing, and he'd begun with the life story of the town's most famous resident—himself. He'd have to write the ending as if it were fiction, though he knew full well it was not. Jane had assured him the project would sell and earn him a substantial amount, but it was a long process, and he needed something in the meantime.

He'd been impatient, thinking he couldn't wait. That he needed an income before he could tell Jane how he truly felt, and knowing he could not, *would not,* wait much longer to make Jane his. If she'd have him, that is.

Shaking his head, he walked downstairs, preparing himself for the worst.

Jane's loins were girded. She stood in a rigid posture when Zach entered the living room, and vowed she wasn't going to take pity on his poor broken heart.

"Coffee?" she said, when he took a seat on the sofa.

"No."

"All right then. I guess I should come right to the point."

"If you don't mind, Jane, I'd like to go first."

She blinked at him, her pretty eyes puzzled. "You would?"

Zach nodded.

"Actually, yes, I do mind. I've been rehearsing this in my mind for hours, and if I don't get it out right now, I never will." Jane paced the length of the living room, walking away from him in brisk strides, her luscious hips swaying as she moved.

Zach pursed his lips. "All right, if you insist. I must admit, you've piqued my curiosity. Whatever could you have to say to me that would require so much preparation?"

She whirled on him. "Damn you, Zachariah Bolton, you have to be the most hardheaded, utterly *dense* man I've ever known."

"Now, wait a minute!" Zach jumped to his feet, intercepting her as she paced back the other way, catching her shoulders in his hands and staring down into her blazing eyes. "I know I've made you angry with me, Jane, and I'm sorry."

"Angry? Zach, you've made me more than angry. This is beyond anger. I want to slap you. The way you've been walking around as if there's a dark cloud over your head ever since you left the last century. I'm sick and tired of watching you pining away for that brainless, air-headed, vapid, overly made-up, self-centered bitch.''

He frowned down at her. She was breathless now, but he could see she was only warming up. "I'm sorry. I'm sorry I let you go on believing I was still pining over Claudia. It was unforgivable, Jane.''

''Yes, dammit, it was! When are you going to wake up and see her for what she is…was, I mean. Zach, she walked out on her own flesh and blood. Not once, but twice. The second time when she had every reason to believe he was on his death bed. How in the name of God can a man as intelligent as you are think he's in love with a woman like that?''

He shrugged. "I don't, Jane I never really did.''

''Well, I'm sick and tired of seeing it, and that's all. I've been waiting and waiting for you to wake up, Zach, because I don't want you to leave me…us. But dammit, I can't stand watching this anymore. I'm twice the woman that Claudia ever was and it's high time you realized it.''

''Ten times, easily.''

''I don't want to…what?'' Jane stopped yelling, drew a breath, and stared up at him.

''I said you're ten times the woman Claudia is. More than that. Perhaps a hundred times, Jane. And I haven't been pining away for her at all. In fact I haven't given her a second thought since we came back here.''

Jane blinked. "You haven't?''

''No, I haven't.''

''Well, then…why have you been…so…''

''Depressed? Ah, Jane, it has nothing to do with

Claudia. Nothing at all, I promise you that." He let his hands fall upon her shoulders, met her eyes fully, so that she could see the sincerity in his own. He didn't want her doubting him. Not ever again. "In fact, there's something you should know. That night, that night she spent in my room. Nothing happened between us, Jane. She wanted it to, but I...I found I simply wasn't interested anymore."

"You weren't?"

He smiled and looked at her. "You sound so amazed, Jane. Did you really believe me that gullible? I knew perfectly well she only came to me because my wealth and standing had suddenly made me desirable in her eyes. And because her wealthy husband died, and left most of his fortune to his nephews. You're right, she's utterly selfish. Her heart is made of solid stone...if she even has one."

"But I don't understand. All this brooding you've been doing—"

"The source was purely financial. I hate being a burden on you and Cody."

"Burden," she snapped, rolling her eyes. "You know better."

He nodded. "I guess I do. It's more than that. Jane, I've been feeling so low because I've been having trouble dealing with the fact that I have nothing to offer you."

"Nothing to..."

"But I've decided to swallow my pride, Jane, because I can't wait any longer to tell you how I feel."

She blinked up at him. "H-how?"

Zach smiled very slightly. "Utterly, madly, completely in love with you," he said softly. "And irrevocably devoted to your son. And determined to make the both of you mine.'' Her lips parted, but no words escaped. ''I know I'm in dire straights right now, Jane, but I won't be. I'm a reasonably intelligent man with a strong back. I'll find a way. I'll dig ditches if I have to, darling, but…''

''I'm so sorry,'' she whispered. And for a moment, his heart stopped, because he thought she was going to turn him down. ''Zach, I'm not sure you're going to forgive me for this…but…''

''But what? You don't feel the same? Jane, you do. I know you do, I see it in your eyes and I feel it when…'' He let his words trail off, because there were no words powerful enough to show her that they were meant to be together. He pulled her closer to him, tight and hard against his body, and he bowed his head, capturing her pliant lips beneath his, kissing her so deeply and so passionately that she couldn't possibly doubt the truth. Heat grew and sizzled in his veins when their tongues met and twined, and her hands threaded into his hair, and she fed hungrily from his mouth.

And at last he lifted his head, met her blazing eyes. ''Don't tell me you don't feel anything for me, Jane,'' he whispered.

''I…I wasn't going to,'' she replied, a bit breathlessly. She stiffened her spine, and gently extricated herself from his grip. ''I'll never tell you that, Zach. But there's something you need to know.''

At her insistence, he released her, but reluctantly.

She went to the coffee table and picked up a stack of aged-looking papers, and when she straightened, she handed them to him. "Here. These belong to you."

"What…" Frowning, Zach took them.

"I found these in the safe that was stored in the attic. The safe itself was an antique, but worthless unless it was usable, of course, so I called a locksmith, when we first moved in. I found these things inside, and tucked them away and forgot about them. I didn't even think of them again until you and Ben came here to stay."

Zach sorted through the papers, nodding in recognition. They belonged to him, all of them. Stocks, savings bonds, investment certificates and the like. "I really don't see what difference is makes, Jane. These are over a century out-of-date, worthless and—"

"They're probably worth a fortune, Zach." She lowered her head, eyes focused on the floor.

"What?"

"Well, most of those banks on the notes are still thriving. Some of those companies you invested in then are multimillion-dollar conglomerates today. Take my word for it, Zach, I know about these things. A century's worth of interest adds up to quite a hefty sum."

Zach shook his head slowly as the information sank in. He held in his hands the very thing he'd been agonizing over for days now. "Jane, for God's sake, why didn't you tell me about this?"

Biting her trembling lower lip, she lifted her gaze to meet his. "Because I didn't want you to leave."

"You—"

"I didn't want to lose you, Zach. I kept telling

myself that if I could just keep you here long enough, maybe you'd start to feel for me, what I...what I feel for you.''

''What you feel for me?'' He realized then, that she still hadn't told him what she did feel for him. And he waited, though far from patiently.

She closed her eyes. ''I was afraid you'd take Benjamin and leave when you realized you had the means. And, well, I love him, too, Zach.''

''Too?''

''Yeah,'' she whispered. ''Too.''

Zach shook his head. She swallowed hard, so hard he heard it, saw the motion of the muscles in her throat as she looked up at him and nodded.

''I've been slowly going insane with wanting you, needing you...*loving* you, Jane Fortune...but I convinced myself I couldn't ask you until I had something to offer—''

''You could've come to me with nothing but the clothes on your back, Zachariah. Don't you realize—'' She blinked fast, took a breath. ''Ask me what?''

''To be my wife, Jane. To be the mother Benjamin has never had, the one he's been wishing for. To let me be a father to Cody. To let me love you for the rest of my life. Will you, Jane?''

He saw her lips tremble, saw her eyes well with tears.

''Say yes!'' two voices shouted in unison.

Zach swung around at the same moment Jane did, to see the two small forms perched on the stairs, watching them. Ben and Cody came the rest of the way down, hesitating at the foot of the stairway, arm in arm. Two curly heads of red hair, two pairs of big green eyes, two freckled faces. Two strong, healthy bodies, one a bit bigger than the other. They were brothers to their souls. They stood grinning, awaiting Jane's reply as breathlessly as Zach was.

"Say yes, Jane," Zach whispered, hooking her chin with a forefinger and drawing her gaze to his once more.

"Yes," she said.

The two boys broke into whoops of triumph and ran to them, shouldering their way between them and forcing them apart. "A dad!" Cody said, rushing into Zach's arms and hugging him hard. "I really have a dad!"

Zach had to swallow past a lump in his throat, and then it became impassable when he glanced up to see Benjamin, his arms linked around Jane's neck as she held him tight. "Can I call you Mommy?" Ben whispered loudly in her ear.

"You'd better," she told him, and her tears flowed unchecked down her cheeks. She met Zach's eyes over the heads of the boys. And he knew his own were probably tearing up, too, but there was no helping it. He gently moved Cody aside, his eyes locked with Jane's as he moved toward her. She set Benjamin down on the floor and came to him. They met, and his arms went around her. He kissed her then, the way he'd been longing to do for so long it seemed like forever.

"Did I mention that I love you, Jane?" he asked her, unsure whether she heard over the joyous shouts of the boys.

"It never hurts to say it again," she told him.

Epilogue

"Well now, Sterling, dear," Kate Fortune said, her eyes twinkling, "Didn't I tell you Jane was going to find her heart's desire in that house? Didn't I?"

"Kate, you know perfectly well you were referring to the antique shop and the old-fashioned atmosphere, not that time-hopping inventor."

"Don't be so sure," she chided.

"Now, Kate, there's no way you could have known all of this would happen," Sterling said softly.

"Don't forget, dear, I lived in that house for a time."

Sterling only gaped for a long moment as Kate waggled her eyebrows. "Are you saying...that you knew...about that doorway through time?"

She only shrugged and moved away. "I'm very, very worried about Natalie, Sterling. I have a feeling she needs me." She tilted her head. "Let's go check on her."

"Kate..." Shaking his head, Sterling began to pace. "Kate, the entire idea is to keep you away from your family. But you insist on hopping from one grandchild to the next like some kind of fairy godmother! I'm trying to keep you alive, dear."

"But I'm having so much fun being dead!" She

winked. "Besides, I've never had so much freedom to meddle without getting caught. It's wonderful, darling. Now come here. Sit down with me and let's make some travel plans. I do believe my darling granddaughter Natalie Fortune has been responsible, reliable, and *lonely,* for just about long enough."

"Perhaps I should send her an anonymous note warning her of the whirlwind that's about to descend on her docile life."

"But it's much more fun when it's a surprise, don't you think?"

"You never fail to surprise me, Kate."

"That's good, Sterling. I only hope I never will."

*   *   *   *   *

FORTUNE'S CHILDREN
continues with
WIFE WANTED
by Christine Rimmer

Available this month

Here's an exciting preview....

WIFE WANTED

Rick Dalton pulled up in front of a two-story house with touches of gingerbread trim in the eaves. Rose trees lined the pebbled walk to the front porch—a deep, inviting porch, furnished with wicker armchairs and love seats. There was even a swing.

"It's perfect," Rick said to his son, Toby.

And just then someone inside decided it was time for rock and roll. *Loud* rock and roll.

Rick couldn't help grinning. "So much for perfection." He recognized the song—"Piece of My Heart."

Rick glanced at Toby, and found his blue eyes just like his own watching him.

"Stay here. I'll see what's going on." Rick had to raise his voice to compete with the tortured wails.

Toby granted his father a tiny nod.

From the house, competing with Janis Joplin's agonized moans, came a dog's howl.

What the hell was going on?

By the time he rang the bell, the dog was yowling as loud and as hard as Janis. And Rick thought he heard another voice, human and female, wailing along. Of course, there was no answer. No one could hear anything over the racket.

The door was unlocked. Stepping inside, Rick

moved toward the sound. He halted on the threshold of an old-fashioned front parlor.

He immediately saw a St. Bernard dog, its massive head tipped back, its throat working enthusiastically to produce an earsplitting approximation of doggy harmony.

Between the door where Rick stood and where the dog yowled, a shapely brunette in a forties spangled cocktail dress and gaudy platform shoes wiggled and wailed. Rick leaned in the doorway, wondering with amusement what she'd do when discovered.

It took a few minutes to find out. The brunette was too involved to realize she'd attracted an audience. But the dog noticed Rick right away. It lowered its huge head. It loped over to Rick and nuzzled him with a large, wet nose. Rick granted the animal a quick scratch.

The woman went right on singing her heart out. Though he'd yet to see her face, she looked great from behind. She shimmied around, no doubt wondering where the dog had gone. She froze in mid-screech when she caught sight of Rick.

"Oh!" Her creamy skin flooded with agonized color. "How long have you been here?" She had to shout to be heard.

Rick did his best to stop grinning. "Long enough," he yelled back.

She made a pained face. "I was afraid you'd say that."

"I rang, but..."

She waved a hand. "Never mind. I understand." She went to turn off the stereo.

"You must be my prospective tenant. Excuse us.

We just...well, Bernie begged me to play Janis, so I did.''

"Bernie," Rick echoed. "That would be the dog?"

"Mm-hmm."

"The dog can talk?"

"Not exactly. But when he wants Janis, he brings me the CD."

"A bright dog."

"Extremely."

Neither of them paid attention as the dog in question wandered out. The woman drew her shoulders back and closed the distance between them, holding out her hand.

"I'm Natalie Fortune."

Rick took her hand. It was soft, a little hot from all that dancing—and a nice fit in his. She smelled of clean sweat and soap and flowers. He introduced himself.

"And there's a little boy, right?"

"Right."

She looked down at their hands and he realized that the handshaking was finished. He released her. She stepped back and gazed at him. She had the most gorgeous brown eyes he'd ever seen. "I, um, thought you'd be here at two."

He glanced at his watch. "I guess I'm a few minutes early."

She smiled. "And I let the time get away from me." Her smile became tender. "Hello."

Rick turned to see Toby hovering inside the door, his mouth quirking upward in response to Natalie's greeting, his hand resting in the ruff of the St. Bernard.

Rick was stunned. His son had actually smiled!

"I see you've met Bernie," she said.

Toby nodded.

"I'm Natalie. What's your name?"

"Toby. His name's Toby," Rick supplied quickly.

Toby reached out and touched one of the bangles on Natalie's dress. A silvery laugh escaped her. "You like?" Taking Toby by the hand, she rose.

At one end of the sofa lay a huge steamer trunk, its lid flung back, various articles of clothing spilling out. Natalie led Toby to it.

"This trunk was my Grandma Kate's," she announced. "I found this fabulous dress in there." She gave Rick a wink.

Kneeling by the trunk, she pulled out a flowered scarf, a wide-brimmed pink hat and a black patent-leather clutch purse, all of which she set on the floor.

She chatted away to Toby and he watched her, his small face rapt.

Then Natalie began dressing the St. Bernard. She slanted the hat just so on the dog's head, tied the scarf around his neck and stuck the purse in his mouth. Then she clapped her hands in delight and declared, "He looks great, don't you think?"

Toby actually nodded. The dog thumped his tail.

Natalie looked up and caught Rick watching. She flashed him a grin, then rose and advised Toby, "Go ahead. Bernie loves to play dress-up." Bernie managed to bark in agreement without dropping the purse. "I'm going to show your father the house."

She moved toward Rick. "Ready for the tour?"

Captivated, Rick heard himself say, "Sure."

She marched past him in her silly shoes. He fell behind her, but couldn't resist one backward glance at his son, who was trying on a helmet and ducking Bernie's tongue.

Natalie led Rick to the foyer and up the stairs first, explaining the finer points of the house as they moved along. Then she stopped near the top of the stairs.

Her brow furrowed. "Is Toby all right?"

Rick tensed. "What do you mean?"

She leaned against the banister. "I mean, is something bothering him? He seems…too quiet. He didn't say a word."

Rick looked away. He'd been in this woman's house for ten minutes, max. She was a stranger. But she didn't *feel* like a stranger. She drew him. And in ten minutes she'd already accomplished the impossible: she'd made his son smile.

He met her eyes. "Toby's mother died several months ago. Toby was in the car when it happened. He hasn't spoken since the accident."

"Oh. I'm so sorry."

"His mother and I were divorced. And I…hadn't seen Toby in a while. That's why I'm interested in this place. We need a little time together, just Toby and me, where he can learn to trust me and I can get to know him better. Does that make sense?"

Those big eyes were full of understanding. "Yes, it does. Perfect sense. Let me show you the rest of the house."

He thought that he could stand here talking to her

forever, but all he said was, "Yes, that's a good idea."

Later they trooped out behind the house and down to the lake. Natalie took Rick out onto a wide dock and into the attached boathouse where a fifty-six-foot houseboat, the *Lady Kate,* was moored.

"This was my grandpa Ben's," Natalie explained fondly, patting the hull of the boat. "She'll be at your disposal during the time you stay here." For a moment those enormous eyes met his.

And he couldn't help thinking that he'd like more than the boat to be at his disposal.

Harlequin Historicals®
Historical Romantic Adventure!

From rugged lawmen and
valiant knights to defiant heiresses
and spirited frontierswomen,
Harlequin Historicals will
capture your imagination with
their dramatic scope, passion
and adventure.

Harlequin Historicals...
they're too good to miss!

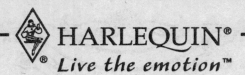

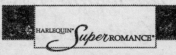

passionate powerful provocative love stories

**Silhouette Desire delivers
strong heroes, spirited heroines
and compelling love stories.**

Desire features your favorite authors,
including

Annette Broadrick,
Ann Major,
Anne McAllister
and Cait London.

**Passionate, powerful and provocative
romances *guaranteed!***

For superlative authors, sensual stories
and sexy heroes, choose Silhouette Desire.

passionate powerful provocative love stories

HARLEQUIN®
INTRIGUE®
WE'LL LEAVE YOU BREATHLESS!

If you've been looking for thrilling tales of
contemporary passion and sensuous love stories
with taut, edge-of-the-seat suspense—then
you'll love Harlequin Intrigue!

Every month, you'll meet six new heroes
who are guaranteed to make your spine tingle
and your pulse pound. With them you'll enter
into the exciting world of Harlequin Intrigue—
where your life is on the line
and so is your heart!

THAT'S INTRIGUE—
ROMANTIC SUSPENSE
AT ITS BEST!

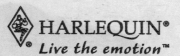

HARLEQUIN®
Live the emotion™